"Let's Get This Straight, Jessica Stephens, Right Here, Right Now,"

Kurt said. "If I ever become a father, I'll do it the old-fashioned way. Skin to naked skin. There won't be any contracts, or doctors, or agreements." His voice dropped a hostile octave. "If I ever have a baby, it will be the result of lovemaking, soft and sweet, hard and fast, but lovemaking, by every definition of the word."

She paled.

"I'd be married, Jessie, and my wife would have my complete and total commitment. There would be no payment, except an emotional one. And that cost would be high. I'd demand everything she had to offer."

Dear Reader,

April brings showers, and this month Silhouette Desire wants to shower you with six new, passionate love stories!

Cait London's popular Blaylock family returns in our April MAN OF THE MONTH title, *Blaylock's Bride*. Honorable Roman Blaylock grapples with a secret that puts him in a conflict between confiding in the woman he loves and fulfilling a last wish.

The provocative series FORTUNE'S CHILDREN: THE BRIDES continues with Leanne Banks's *The Secretary and the Millionaire*, when a wealthy CEO turns to his assistant for help in caring for his little girl.

Beverly Barton's next tale in her 3 BABIES FOR 3 BROTHERS miniseries, *His Woman, His Child*, shows a rugged heartbreaker transformed by the heroine's pregnancy. Powerful sheikhs abound in *Sheikh's Ransom*, the Desire debut title of Alexandra Sellers's dramatic new series, SONS OF THE DESERT. A marine gets a second chance at love in *Colonel Daddy*, continuing Maureen Child's popular series BACHELOR BATTALION. And in Christy Lockhart's *Let's Have a Baby!*, our BACHELORS AND BABIES selection, the hero must dissuade the heroine from going to a sperm bank and convince her to let *him* father her child—the old-fashioned way!

Allow Silhouette Desire to give you the ultimate indulgence— all six of these fabulous April romance books!

Enjoy!

Joan Marlow Golan
Senior Editor, Silhouette Desire

Please address questions and book requests to:
Silhouette Reader Service
U.S.: 3010 Walden Ave., P.O. Box 1325, Buffalo, NY 14269
Canadian: P.O. Box 609, Fort Erie, Ont. L2A 5X3

LET'S HAVE A BABY!
CHRISTY LOCKHART

SILHOUETTE *Desire*
Published by Silhouette Books
America's Publisher of Contemporary Romance

SILHOUETTE BOOKS

ISBN 0-373-76212-7

LET'S HAVE A BABY!

Copyright © 1999 by Christine Pacheco

Printed in U.S.A.

Books by Christy Lockhart

Silhouette Desire

Hart's Baby #1193
Let's Have a Baby! #1212

Previously published under Christine Pacheco

Silhouette Desire

The Rogue and the Rich Girl #960
Lovers Only #1054
A Husband in Her Stocking #1113

CHRISTY LOCKHART

married her real-life hero, Jared, who proved to her that dreams really do come true. They live in Colorado with their two children, Raymond and Whitney.

Christy remembers always wanting to be a writer. She even talked her elementary school librarian into "publishing" her books. She notes always preferring romances because they're about that special moment when dreams are possible and the future is a gift to unfold.

You can write to Christy at P.O. Box 448, Eastlake, CO 80614.

With thanks, as always,
to Pamela Johnson and Lisa Craig
for invaluable input and insight.

Also dedicated to Ray and Alice Pacheco, the best
in-laws a woman could be blessed with. Thanks for
helping me figure out what love is all about....

Prologue

Columbine Crossing Courier
"Around the Town" by Miss Starr

Could our very own bookkeeper, Jessica Stephens, be knitting baby booties after work hours?

Rumor has it that Jessica was seen at the general store purchasing pink and blue yarn, knitting needles and several patterns for baby clothing. To Miss Starr's knowledge, Jessica has no nieces or nephews, and that can only mean one thing....

I wonder who's the lucky father? This may be Columbine Crossing's best kept secret, besides Miss Starr's identity!

I'll be back next week, faithful readers. Your intrepid reporter promises to bring you the name of the baby's father.

For now, this is all the news you can use.

Miss Starr surreptitiously glanced around the post office, making sure she was alone before clipping her article from the *Courier*. She never kept the originals, so no one would discover who was Miss Starr's real-life counterpart.

After patting the neat bun at her nape, she slid the newsprint into a folder, then locked it in the filing cabinet.

Mercy. Jessica Stephens? Possibly pregnant? Who would have believed it? It amazed Miss Starr that Jessica had been able to keep the bloom of true love hidden for this long.

Miss Starr frowned, wondering who the father might be. It certainly was a mystery! Her frown faded, replaced by a grin. There was little that gave her more pleasure than solving a good mystery...especially where love was concerned.

After all, having been born on Valentine's Day some sixty years ago—she never said just how many years—she was the small mountain town's self-appointed Cupid. Not only that, but now that Miss Starr had a newspaper column, she had an obligation to keep the town's residents informed.

And she took her responsibilities seriously, indeed.

Moving in front of the post office's large window, she glanced down the street toward the church.

In her opinion, it had been far too long since the bells rang out for a wedding—almost two years if her memory was correct...which it most certainly was.

The town's welcome sign wavered in the cold, early spring wind gusting from the tip of Eagle's Peak, some 14,000 feet high. The sign listed the town's population at 972 people. If Jessie were indeed pregnant, the sign would need to be changed to 973.

Nothing could make Miss Starr happier.

One

"*You want me to what?*" Shock and disbelief propelled Kurt Majors to his feet.

Jessie Stephens winced, then licked her lower lip.

Jaw clenched, he stared at her, unable to believe he'd heard right.

After a shaky exhalation, Jessie bravely looked at him. "I realize this comes as a surprise to you—"

"Surprise?" he interrupted, shock now turning to anger. "Lady, surprise doesn't come close."

"Please, just hear me out."

He raised his hand to stop her, but she ignored him, tipping back her chin to unflinchingly meet his gaze.

"I've thought about this a lot, Kurt. I know it seems sudden, but I promise you, I've looked at all the angles and considered all the options. This isn't a spur of the moment decision."

Jessie blinked several times, then hurried on. "You're the perfect man to father my child."

"The answer's no, Jessie."

"Kurt, you once told me that if I needed anything, *anything,* you'd be there for me, no questions asked."

"For God's sake, Jessie, the offer didn't include getting you pregnant."

She twirled her thumbs together. From years of knowing her, he recognized the nervousness in the gesture. After long moments, she looked at him again, pleading eyes connecting with the hardness of his stare.

A lesser man might have folded right then.

After stilling her motions, she spoke quietly, "I believed you were a man of your word."

A pulse ticked in his temple. "Are you questioning my integrity?"

Wisely she took a step backward and shook her head vehemently. "No. Never."

The fire crackled, punctuating the quiet. Jessie jumped.

"Won't work, Jessie. I'm not into manipulation. You should know better."

"I'm making a mess of this." Obviously trying to gather her thoughts, she stalled for time, pushing dark blond bangs back from her forehead. "I don't want you to think this is all about me, that I'm expecting you to do this for free."

She'd lost her mind.

He'd always admired her bravery and the way she thought things through. That was, until right now.

The ticking in his temple became an all-out throb.

"I'm willing to do your books for the next five years at no charge if you'll do me this one favor."

"You're going to pay me to get you pregnant?"

Silence thundered and tension sparked.

"I wouldn't put it that way, exactly."

Keeping time with the fury flashing through him, Kurt drummed his fingers on the mantel in an ominous staccato. Then, as tension tightened to a snapping point, he stopped. "How would you put it, Jessie?"

She spoke slowly, as if measuring her words. "I see it more like we're helping each other, you know, mutual benefit."

"Stud service for bookkeeping." He pounded his fist on the mantel. "Nice ring to it."

She retreated farther, until her back connected with the windowsill. The width of the ranch house's large living room separated them, and it wasn't enough space.

Her fingers were laced, and her knuckles had whitened. "That's not how it is."

He debated whether or not he should throw her out. Before he reached a decision, she plowed ahead once more, her tenacity matched only by her insanity.

"This is a smart business arrangement for you," she insisted, her words wavering.

Tears thickened her voice. He watched her choke them back as he'd seen her do so many times in childhood.

"You've been paying me to do the ranch's books for a couple of years. We both know that in order for you to grow and meet your projections, you need to hire at least one more hand. I make enough money from my other customers, so I can afford to do yours free. If you don't have to pay me, you'll have extra money to achieve your goals."

"You've got it all figured out," he all but snarled.

"This is perfect. Don't you see, Kurt?"

"No, I don't." He started drumming his fingers again. She'd been right about one thing. She had thought through all the angles. Didn't matter. Wrong was wrong. Nothing would make him change the moral beliefs encoded in his DNA. "Dress it up any way you want, Jessie. Disguise it and try and make it more palatable. All you want from me is stud service."

"Okay, Kurt. If that's what you want to call it."

His eyes narrowed. She actually thought she could convince him to reduce the act of lovemaking to a business decision, as if bringing a baby into the world was a commodity to be bought and sold, balanced on some ledger.

Damn her and her determination.

Jessie, the girl he'd looked out for, the teen he'd protected, the woman he did volunteer work with, wanted to take their years of friendship and working together and smash them, making them something cheap and tawdry, something she could get from any man.

"Will you do it?" Her whisper was soft, hopeful. "For me?"

Fury licked at his insides, the same way the fire licked at the log it greedily consumed in the grate. "Assuming I was foolish enough to agree to this lunacy, Jessie, how did you plan on us going about the act? Inviting me over for coffee and sex?"

Color rushed into her face, then drained, leaving her pale.

"Were you planning to slip into something comfortable and asking me to join you in the bedroom? How about a glass of wine first, to settle your nerves? No, probably not. That might not be good for the baby."

"Kurt—"

She'd pushed him beyond reason. Demolishing the distance between them, he locked his hands around her shoulders. He captured her gaze and refused to let it go.

"Were you going to undress me or was I going to have to take off my own clothes? And how about you, Jessie? As part of the bargain would I at least get to watch you strip?" His gaze flicked to the top button on her blouse. "Or maybe you'd figured I'd get to take your clothes off. After all, I should get some enjoyment out of it, shouldn't I?"

He moved one of his hands to the place where a pulse wildly beat in her throat. Then, with his finger, he circled the button he'd looked at. "Time is money, everything is money, isn't it, Jessie?"

"Kurt, you're being ridiculous," she said breathlessly. For a moment, her gaze hypnotically rested on his hand.

"So maybe you were just going to be naked when I arrived so we could get on with the show."

He unfastened the button and allowed the silk shirt to slip apart. Intention clear, he placed his fingertip in the opening. "Is this what you want? Tell me, Jess. You've supposedly thought everything through. Clue me in."

The rush of their heartbeats roared over the fireplace.

"Kurt, don't do this."

"Stud service comes with expectations. Would you like a wham-bam-thank-you, ma'am, or shall we take it slower, a seduction, say? Where will we do it? In the bedroom? Or we can make it easy and just use the living room."

He cut a purposeful glance over his shoulder. "Better yet, we could drop down and go for it right there on the couch. How 'bout it, Jessie? You want the top or do you prefer the bottom?"

Tears swam at the corners of her eyes. "This isn't like you. You're being crude."

"That's what you want, isn't it, Jessie? My sperm? Nothing else matters. Since you've worked out all the details of my payment, you'll probably have a contract you want me to sign.

"Oh, and dates. I'll expect a calendar with your most fertile days circled, that way we can schedule our sexual rendezvous. Or we could just go at it for an entire month. I wrap up most of my ranch work around dusk. I could come for dinner and stay as long as it took."

Her outrageous proposal had struck at the heart of his principles. Men were meant to be lovers, providers, helpmates, spouses, protectors...fathers.

They weren't supposed to be disposable, interchangeable donors.

To have her throw his ideals and beliefs in his face rankled. She saw him as a means to her ends. She'd stung his pride, oh yeah, but so much more. She'd taken everything he prided and defiled it.

Jessie still had a thing or two to learn about life.

Before he taught them to her, here and now, he moved his hand, curving it around her shoulder again. "What happens if you don't get pregnant right away? Will you want to keep sleeping together? How long shall we give it? Two months? Three? Six?"

"You've misunderstood this whole thing." A furious blush painted her cheeks. "We, er, wouldn't need to actually, you know…"

Jessie's voice trailed off as his brows drew together sharply.

"Go on." *If you dare.*

Kurt wondered if Jessie realized how tenuous his hold on his temper truly was. The ends were fraying, threatening to unravel, or worse, snap completely.

"You're hurting me."

"Sorry." He wasn't. Nor did he loosen his grip.

She averted her gaze.

"Look at me, Jessie. You're asking me to get you pregnant. Face those realities, if nothing else."

Her lips were parted slightly and he noticed the tip of her tongue. Pink and moist.

Jeez.

Why the hell was he noticing little things about her now? That was the last thing he wanted to do. She'd insulted him, trespassed on the grounds of their friendship, tried to buy his services.

He shouldn't be noticing her as a desirable woman.

But he was noticing just that…the sight of her perfectly shaped lips, the softness of her skin, the feel of her in his arms, the fact that she smelled as fresh as a stroll through a rain-washed meadow.

Dark blond hair teased her face and shoulders. Absently

he wondered how the strands would feel against his chest. Silky and sexy?

Unconsciously his hold tightened. Stifling a gasp, she dragged her lower lip between her teeth. Kurt forced his fingers to relax.

Never before in his life had he touched a woman in anger, not even when Belinda betrayed him. With a few, well-placed words, Jessie had changed all that, goading him into something he hadn't known he was capable of.

She finally followed his instructions, looking up at him. Her wide eyes and luminous gaze asked for something unspoken. Understanding, compassion maybe. In that moment, he was capable of granting neither.

"There's a clinic in Denver," she said quietly.

When he didn't respond, she cleared her throat. "I can get pregnant without..."

"Yes?" He barely managed the word.

"There's this procedure that you can do in the doctor's office... You could go one day and I can go there another..." Color suddenly swamped her face again, obliterating even the traces of her makeup. "I'm saying that we wouldn't actually have to make love or anything."

"Wouldn't have to..." He trailed off and reality sliced through him, as if he'd plowed headlong into barbed wire. *"You want me to do it in a cup?"*

She put her hands in supplicate against his chest. "Kurt, wait, I didn't mean to insult you."

Insulted barely began to define it. Blood thundered through him, demanding action. "You don't want a man, a marriage, or even a relationship. You don't want me. All you want is my donation? At a *clinic?* In a *cup?*"

She winced.

Fury threatened to devour everything and everyone in his path. "Let's get this straight, Jessica Stephens, right here, right now. The answer's no. Not just no, but hell, no.

"If I ever become a father, I'll do it the old-fashioned way. Skin to naked skin.

"There won't be any contracts, or doctors, or agreements." His voice dropped by a hostile octave. "If I ever have a baby, it will be the result of lovemaking, soft and sweet, hard and fast, but lovemaking, by every definition of the word."

She paled.

"I'd be married, Jessie, and my wife would have my complete and total commitment. There would be no payment, except an emotional one. And that cost would be high. I'd demand everything she had to offer

"We'd take off each other's clothes, and when my finger touched her here..." He illustrated, opening a second button on Jessie's blouse.

She drew in her breath sharply and he continued, "Yeah, just like that, she'd react like that, and more. She'd reach for my belt buckle and we would tumble onto the bed together."

His callused finger grazed the skin right above the clasp that joined her bra. Her eyes widened.

"I'd bring her to a climax, listen to her call out my name." Rather than diminish, his anger continued to simmer. "Any baby of mine will be conceived when I'm buried deep inside my wife. There will be mutual love and passion, and it will create life.

"It'll be more than just sex, and a hell of a lot more than what you want."

Silence crackled.

"You asked the wrong man."

With that, he released her and watched her shoulders slump. He hardened his heart against the tears clinging to her eyelashes.

"Kurt..." She swiped at the tears. "I understand what you're saying." Her words were rushed and unsure. "If the only way you'd agree is if we did it, you know, the old-fashioned way, then I guess we could.''

Just what he wanted. A martyr in his bed.

"You didn't understand a word I said," he snapped. Kurt grabbed at his self-control. He strode to the far side of the room, where the fire feasted on a log. "Forget it, Jessie."

She lowered her head and hid her expression.

"If you thought I could do this, Jessie, you don't know me."

Humiliation flooded over her. "No." Jessie mentally cursed her voice for cracking and betraying her inner emotions. "I guess I don't."

Her fingers shook as she refastened the buttons he'd opened. Her skin burned where he'd touched her, making the mortification complete. She could barely breathe, let alone speak. Words rough and scratchy, she fumbled over an apology.

Since he was on the other side of the room, Jessie seized the opportunity to flee, rushing from his study, then yanking open the front door and dragging it shut behind her.

The tears that had threatened to spill for the past fifteen minutes now curtained her eyes.

She'd always known no man would ever want her.

Sam, her ex-fiancé, had reinforced that knowledge, a hundred times.

How could she have been foolish enough to believe Kurt was any different? Even though they wouldn't have actually had to sleep together, no man would willingly get her pregnant.

She ran toward her car, praying she could outdistance the pain of his rejection.

"Jessie! Wait!"

She didn't.

As long as she lived, she'd never be able to face Kurt again. Even worse was the knowledge that she'd destroyed their friendship.

The first of the tears chased down her cheeks and the cold Colorado night air froze them to her skin. She struggled to slide the key into the ignition only to have the set slip from her grip and tumble to the floorboard.

Frustration drowning all other emotions, she slapped her hand against the steering wheel.

Nothing had gone right since she arrived at Kurt's.

Stupid, stupid.

She shouldn't have done this, should have just stuck with her original plan.

Wasting precious moments, she switched on the interior light to search for the keys. Just as Kurt reached for the car door, determination written on his rigid features, she managed to turn the ignition.

Blinking desperately to clear her blurry vision, she put the car in gear and floored the accelerator.

In the rearview mirror she saw Kurt, reflected by the porch light. Then he slammed his fist into his open palm as Jessie sped away. His brows were set in a scowl and his jaw hardened.

She barely slowed down before turning onto the gravel road leading back to town and home.

Ten minutes later, she rushed into the house, clicking the dead bolt securely into place before her shoulders collapsed against the door.

Kurt hadn't followed her.

Even though she'd checked the mirror a dozen times, she hadn't seen a single set of lights on the inky mountain road.

She was alone, just as she wanted.

A lump clogged Jessie's throat, and she wondered if she would ever stop lying to herself.

She'd never wanted to be alone. Her entire life, she'd wanted to love and be loved. But not even her own mother cared enough to keep her. Nor had the series of foster parents. She'd spent night after night praying that someone would adopt her, keep her, make her feel as though she were part of a family instead of facing the world all alone.

And every night, she'd turned off the light, thinking that tomorrow, maybe tomorrow, things would be different.

Jessie told herself that Kurt's rejection didn't surprise her, that she'd expected he'd refuse. So, why then, did she hurt so much?

Trying to bury the pain of tonight's confrontation, she shoved away from the door. Her suitcase sat in the foyer, still packed. Now, more than ever, she wished she'd just left well enough alone and had never given in to the temptation of approaching Kurt.

Yet, every night since she made the appointment a few weeks ago, she'd dreamed of knowing the baby's father instead of just receiving an anonymous donation.

As she trailed her fingertips across the suitcase's zipper, she realized that every time in her life that she had dared to dream, she had been hurt.

It wouldn't ever happen again, she vowed. She was done fantasizing. With his cold words, Kurt had reinforced the danger of believing.

This time, she vowed, she'd learned the lesson and learned it well. It was safer to stick to facts and reality. Maybe life would be less painful that way.

Soon, she would have the baby she'd always wanted, holding it, cuddling and snuggling. For the first time in her life, she would know and give unconditional love.

Protectively she placed her palm across her abdomen.

Nothing and no one would stand in her way.

With resolution, she squared her shoulders and crossed into the bedroom. But the instant she unfastened the top button of her shirt, memories flooded her.

It had been so long since she'd been touched. The feel of Kurt's work-roughened skin against her smooth skin had sent shivers of something she didn't dare name skating down her spine to settle near her womb.

For a moment, if she closed her eyes and imagined, she might believe that he'd actually *wanted* to touch her....

But he hadn't.

He'd simply been trying to drive home his angry point. As she'd learned, wanting and being wanted were for other women.

Jessie finished undressing and pulled on a flannel nightdress. Last week, at the women's clothing store in town, she'd passed satin and lace teddies on the way to the dressing room. She'd stopped, looking longingly at the material while wondering how it might feel against her skin.

Since it didn't really matter anyway, she'd settled for flannel. No one would see her in lingerie. Besides, a long gown was warmer, especially when there was no one to share the bed with.

After combing her hair its customary one hundred strokes, she turned off the lights and slipped beneath cold blankets, curling into a ball, seeking protection from the rejection still searing her heart.

Seconds later, the insistent thud of a fist on her front door made her sit upright.

"Open up, Jessie!"

Kurt.

She dragged a pillow against her chest and hugged it tight. Maybe if she ignored him...

"I'll get Sheriff McCall, say we've got an emergency."

He wouldn't.

"I will, Jessie. Try me."

Her heart pounded.

"Neighbors just turned on their porch light."

Jessie groaned. Maybe when she went to Denver in the morning, she wouldn't come back.

"No, Mrs. Johnson, Jessie's not answering. I'm starting to worry. Yes, her car's here."

Silence hung as cold as a newborn snow.

"Sure...thanks. I'll wait here for the sheriff."

"Wait!" Galvanized by the threat, Jessie tossed back the covers and pillow, then ran toward the front door. She'd never be able to show her face in Columbine Crossing again if anyone else witnessed her private torment. "Don't you dare call Spencer," she called, twisting the bolt.

Before she had a chance to open the door, Kurt did.

She gasped.

He stood there, wearing no jacket, his cheeks bitten by the frost. His breath clung frigidly to the night air, air that still felt more like winter than spring.

"Invite me in."

"But the neighbors—"

"Are asleep. Invite me in, Jessie."

There were no lights on across the street. There was only Kurt, all six feet of him, masculine determination written in the set of his jaw and shoulders.

Jessie had never felt more helpless. "You lied."

"I accomplished my goal." When she said nothing more, he added, "Fine. We'll talk here."

In the years she'd known him, she'd learned to tell when he was joking. He wasn't. "Kurt…"

"Decision's yours, Jessie. We're going to talk. Now. We can do it inside or out here, where the neighbors might overhear. Unless you want what I have to say printed in Miss Starr's column?"

The threat chilled as much as the weather. For protection against both, she dragged the neckline of her nightie tighter around her throat. The subzero wind nipped at her toes and ankles. But even that didn't freeze as much as the ice in Kurt's green eyes.

"Okay," he said. "We'll play it your way. First of all—"

"Stop!" Her insides reeled and she felt as though the world had started spinning backward. "You can come in." The invitation contained only the barest hint of civility.

He didn't hesitate.

With the door closed and both of them standing in the tiny foyer, she suddenly felt very small, very feminine. Her skin tingled where he'd touched her earlier, and sanity demanded that she get him out of here immediately. "Go ahead, Kurt. Say what you need to so you can leave."

"I'm wondering," he said, taking a step toward her, filling her senses and indicating her suitcase with his thumb. "Where the hell you think you're going."

The question was delivered quietly, but whipped by the lash of anger.

Jessie took another step away from him, then stopped. She reminded herself he was her best friend's brother, nothing more. She was a grown woman and answered only to herself.

Straightening her spine, she pretended an indifference she didn't feel. "It's none of your business."

"You made it my business."

She shook her head, her hair falling forward to frame her face and allowing her to hide. "Look, Kurt, I presented you with a business arrangement, but you didn't like the terms. End of discussion."

"It would be, if you weren't planning a trip."

Frustration began as a small knot in her stomach. "It's late, and I have to get up early."

"So you can go to Denver."

"Yes."

"And get inseminated."

The knot became tighter. She hated the emphasis he put on the words, as though she was doing something repulsive. Tipping back her head, she gave him a falsely sweet smile. "Good night, Kurt."

He turned and she experienced a flash of triumph.

Then he clicked the dead bolt into place with a threatening thud.

Her heart momentarily stopped. "What are you doing?"

"Stopping you from doing something you'll regret."

Two

Until that moment, Kurt hadn't realized how deadly serious he was.

He knew Jessie, better than she realized. Mary, his sister, had spent many evenings telling him about her friend. He knew about Jessie's broken engagement and the time she was stood-up for the prom.

And because he and Jessie volunteered together at the local children's center, he knew how much having a real family meant to her. But this wasn't the way to accomplish that, no matter what she thought.

"You can't stop me from going to Denver."

"Yes," he said. "I can. And I will. I'll save you from yourself, Jessie."

Slowly she shook her head, loose hair framing her face and so very nearly distracting him.

"Thanks for the offer, but I don't want a knight in shining armor."

"Tough. You've got one."

Her eyes, columbine blue and frosted by icy resolve, seemed to challenge him. "Heroes are for fairy tales, Kurt, just like happily ever afters."

"You don't believe in them."

"No...I never did."

"Never?" he asked. Her eyes told a different story, though. They revealed what she never willingly would.

He took a single step toward her and watched her retreat. It wasn't much, just a fraction of an inch. But her toes, with an intriguing brush of pink across the nails, had peeked out from beneath her nightclothes.

The flannel gown, severe, prim and proper, swooshed around her ankles. More than that, however, it was her eyes that still riveted his attention. They hinted at the secrets in her soul. "Never, not even once? In all your childhood years, you never wanted to be rescued?"

She opened her mouth, then closed it again.

"You were content with what you had, being shuffled from family to family?"

"Get out." She pointed to the door.

"A little close to the truth?" he asked with coiled quietness. Her ridiculous proposal had angered him, the fact that she wanted only his sperm infuriated him and now her determination to go to Denver fanned a flame of frustration in him.

"Truth?" she repeated. "You want the truth, Kurt? Well, how's this?" Her voice quivered, betraying the emotions that Kurt knew she was trying to hide. "I'm going to have a baby—if not yours, then someone else's. So save us both the aggravation of misplaced chivalry."

He shook his head and advanced again. "Sorry, sweetheart. *You* brought this to me and *you* made it my concern."

"So what are you going to do, physically stop me from leaving in the morning?"

"If I have to."

She shivered.

He took another, measured step toward her.

"You can't be serious."

"Try me."

She sucked in a breath, her breasts rising beneath the cotton of her gown. Her nipples strained against the fabric and something deep inside him wrenched. For the first time since he'd first met her—when she wore a braid and knee-high white socks with a skirt—she affected him in a way that had nothing to do with friendship.

His instincts warned of danger while his body urged him toward it.

He reminded himself that Jessie was his sister's friend.

Yeah. Right. Too bad he wasn't buying what his mind was selling.

"This is crazy, impossible."

For a second, he had no idea what she was talking about.

"If you stop me in the morning, I'll go later, after you leave. You can't hold me prisoner in my own home forever."

"Is that a challenge?"

"Kurt, stop this ridiculousness."

"Sure." He folded his arms. Better than touching her. "As soon as you agree to cancel your appointment."

"If it'll get you out of here, I promise I'll call the clinic first thing in the morning."

"Not good enough."

Her eyelids squeezed shut for a fraction of a second.

"I'll cancel it for you."

"Cancel it for me? You're out of your ever-loving mind."

"That makes two of us. Give me the number of the doctor's office, Jessie. Then I'll leave you alone to your sweet dreams."

"And an empty house," she said quietly, the words more of a confession than a statement.

She winced, obviously having disclosed more than she wanted. He should pretend he hadn't heard, and more, hadn't seen the painful display of honesty in her eyes.

But right now, Kurt wasn't feeling like much of a gentleman. He'd capitalize on her weakness, get her to see things his way, the right way. "That's what this is all about, isn't it?" he asked quietly. "An empty house."

She didn't answer him.

"If you don't like being alone, get married."

"Sure. Which of my many suitors should I choose?"

Bitterness tainted her question. Pain lay there in her voice, raw and exposed. Before he reacted to it, she rushed away from him toward the back of the house, leaving him alone. He knew he'd said something wrong, but exactly what, he wasn't sure.

Women. What did he know about them anyway? Not enough, if his divorce was anything to judge by.

Still, Jessie was hurting and remnants of her earlier pain lingered in her gaze. He was on the right track.

Kurt hadn't been much interested in the fairy tales his mother had read to him and Mary. He, too, believed that chivalry had died an untimely death, if it had ever existed outside of books.

But that didn't give him the power to leave Jessie alone. Something had brought her to him, in the cold, dark hours of an early April evening. Like it or not, as he'd told her earlier, when she reached out to him, she'd involved him.

Jessie had crossed into the kitchen. She stared out the

window, into the desolate expanse of a still-dormant yard, her back to him in a sign of dismissal.

He ignored it.

In the entryway, he propped a shoulder against the doorjamb.

Even though he didn't speak, she asked, "Are you still here?"

He'd had more promising beginnings with women. Somehow, though, nothing else had ever seemed this important. "Tell me about it, Jessie. Talk to me."

Slowly, oh so slowly, the gown swishing, she turned around. Silence, unbroken by anything except their breathing, seemed to simmer.

"What do you want to hear? About the loneliness? Or the way my arms ache to hold a baby? The way I dream, every night, of having a child of my own?"

"How about the way you want to make up for what you didn't have?"

She flinched, as if he'd slapped her.

"I've seen you with the kids at the center. You love them," he said by way of an apology. "Most of us volunteer once a week, but you're there almost every day, aren't you?"

"They need the help."

He nodded. "What about Jessie?" Closing in, he added, "What do you need?"

"I already told you. I need a child of my own."

"Not this way."

She looked up at him, layers of dark blond falling away from her face and revealing a side of her he'd never imagined until tonight. She'd always been tough, never vulnerable; independent, never needy. It was all there, though. It compelled him, made him want to protect her.

"What do you care, Kurt?"

Once, maybe, he might not have. Now, hearing the edge of pain in her tone, watching the shadows beneath her eyes and seeing the defeat in the curve of her shoulders, he cared.

He moved into the warmth of the room, realizing Jessie didn't radiate the same welcome. With the toe of his boot, he hooked a chair leg and dragged it toward him. He sat on the chair backward, arms folded across the top. Whether she knew it or not, it promised to be a long night.

He didn't intend to leave until he got what he wanted: answers, a telephone number and her sworn promise.

If there was one thing that took equal importance with his ranch and his family, it was winning.

"Mary always said you were stubborn."

He looked at her. "She said the same thing about you."

"Me?" Her eyes widened. "I'm not stubborn."

He didn't respond.

"I'm not," she insisted.

"Give me the phone number, Jessie. Get this over with."

"You know I can't do that."

"Then tell me where a husband fits into this picture."

She shook her head and her hair once again fell in gentle disarray around her face. Kurt had to resist the inclination to run his fingers through the tousled strands, discovering for himself if it was as soft as it looked.

"I don't need a man, any man."

"That's harsh."

"Maybe," she conceded. "But so is reality."

She hadn't come any closer to him, but unlike at his house and in her foyer, here she couldn't escape except by getting past him. That wasn't likely to happen. "A broken engagement isn't a good reason to swear off men."

"Yes, it is."

It was back, that ghost of pain in her eyes. He wanted to vanquish it. "Samuel Bucket was a jerk."

"You're not going to get an argument from me."

"Not all men are."

"Really?"

He expected to hear sarcasm in the word. It wasn't there. Instead it was a simple, honest question. "Take me, for example."

"Okay," she said. "Let's take you. You barge into my house when I'm already in bed, lie about the neighbors watching us, lie about calling Sheriff McCall."

Kurt raised a brow.

"Not only that, but you've made something that's none of your concern into some sort of personal quest. And you refuse to leave." Then quietly, she added, "How do you define the word *jerk?*"

He winced, the barb finding its mark. "Not by your standards."

"Obviously."

Kurt gave thanks for the distance between them. The sides of the chair back carved into his thighs. He liked the dig of pain. It distracted him, prevented him from ending this conversation in a way she wouldn't like.

"I'm your sister's friend," she said. "Nothing more. Please, just let it go."

He'd given himself the same argument earlier, telling himself he had no right to get involved. Hadn't washed any better then than it did now. "By default, Jessie, that makes you my friend. You do my books, making you my employee, and we volunteer together at the center. Add in the fact you asked for a personal donation for your cause, and I say I've got more than a casual interest."

"All that's true, so you of all people should understand why this is important to me."

"And you of all people should see why this is insane," he countered.

"I don't."

"Kids need two parents."

Her chin was set at a defiant tilt, another side he'd never seen from her. "They need someone to love them."

"Feed that line to someone else, not to me. I don't buy it. If kids only needed one person, they wouldn't be at the center looking for something they could get at home."

"Problem is, Kurt, those kids don't have parents like I would be. Those parents are often overworked, stressed and burned-out. They have nothing left to give."

"And you're different?"

"I am. I've got a lot of experience from being at the center. You know as well as I do that I work from home. I'll be there all day, every day. There won't be day care or a lot of baby-sitters. A lot of two-parent families aren't that lucky. My schedule can fit my baby's."

In her hands, conviction was a powerful weapon.

"I will be a great mother, give my child all he needs." She paused, a small, private smile playing at the corner of her lips. "Or all she needs."

Breath escaped his lungs. He'd hoped to see that expression—one of softness and maternal expectation—on Belinda's face. The opposite had occurred when he'd broached the subject of starting their family.

She'd frowned, pursing her lips and stating, quite frankly, that she had no intention of ever sharing her body with another human being.

That had been the beginning of the end.

The rest had come when he found out that her assertion hadn't been exactly accurate. She might not have wanted to share her body with a baby, but she'd had no compunction about sharing her intimacies with a man other than her husband.

Kurt was a fast learner and he'd sure as hell learned from the mistake of marriage.

"I can be a good parent, can't you see, Kurt?"

He regarded Jessie, missing nothing. The fire in her eyes had replaced despair. Again, something new. Passion. Amazing. He'd seen Samuel Bucket in a bar the night he and Jessie broke up. Bucket had called her the Ice Princess.

No way. Fire and ice didn't mix. And tonight Kurt had been singed by the fire in her eyes.

"Things will be perfect," she said.

"One person can't be all things to another human being."

"I can and will."

Kurt forced himself to stay in his chair. The urging to get up, grab hold of her and shake some sense into her ran rampant through him, demanding action.

Unconsciously his hands formed fists. "Wait a while. Wait until you find a man."

"I've already tried."

Her lids shuttered her eyes temporarily, and when she opened them again, the transformation stunned him. He'd been right earlier, fire and ice didn't mix. Ice extinguished fire. It also dimmed her blue eyes, clouding them like the leading edge of a storm obscured a mountain peak.

"You rejected me."

Shrapnel landed in his heart. "You can't think—"

"I offered myself to you." She gulped at a breath of air. "You turned me down."

Good God. She thought it was personal. "Look, Jess—"

"It's okay, Kurt. I shouldn't have expected you to put yourself out for me. You were right, I wasn't thinking straight. Why do you think I made an appointment at a clinic?"

He inhaled sharply. "Because you can't get a man?"

"Because no man wants me." Tears once again welled in her eyes. "And because I don't need a man to be whole and complete."

Beneath her bravado, he heard the woven strands of uncertainty and disbelief.

He stood, shoving aside the chair. "You're a desirable woman."

"Of course I am. Hollywood calls at least once a week."

If he was on the wrong end of a branding iron, he'd a whole lot more sure what to do than he was right now.

"Now if you'll excuse me, it's obvious I need my beauty sleep."

He reached out and clamped his hand around her upper arm when she tried to brush past him. "I'm not leaving."

"The couch is lumpy."

It was back…the fire he'd glimpsed earlier. She was a paradox and that intrigued him. He wouldn't leave now, no matter what common sense encouraged.

"Good night, Kurt."

Reluctantly he released her.

Gathering the hem of her gown, she hurried away. The slam of her bedroom door echoed through the small house and all the way down into his gut.

He'd run headlong into a situation he didn't begin to comprehend. He disliked the feeling, and that left him only one option—he had to work the puzzle, look at all the pieces from each angle. He had to figure out what the hell had gotten into Jessie. Then he had to figure out how to get her out of it.

Yeah. It promised to be a long night. Even longer, he realized when he glanced at the couch. She hadn't lied. It was lumpy. Too short, understuffed and lumpy. And she hadn't gotten him a blanket.

Served him right.

His mother often warned him of the penalties for trying to run someone else's life.

Kurt pulled off his boots and dropped them near the end of the couch. He stretched out, tucked his hands behind his neck and stared at the ceiling.

Jessie needed him, even if she didn't know it.

She moved around in the bedroom, the whispers of her actions carrying in the stillness. Deprived of the sight of her, his memory seeped in to fill the void.

He saw Jessie, beseeching him to agree to her crazy idea, the way she dipped her head when he turned her down and the way her lips curled when she argued with him.

Superimposed over the top were images of her looking at him, her smile secretly sensual, her fingers feathering into silky strands of hair and a spark of passion in her eyes that made his insides constrict.

She was rich and complex, desirable, vulnerable, feminine and in need of a protector.

In need of him.

Kurt shifted.

He hadn't thought of himself as anyone's protector, particularly a woman who wouldn't welcome it.

Adjusting his jeans, he wondered why the hell a man who didn't believe in chivalry was being driven by exactly that.

"Going somewhere?"

Jessie froze, her hand curved around the handle of her suitcase. With her heart hammering in her throat, speech was out of the question. Reluctantly releasing her hold, she slowly turned toward him.

He stood in the entry to the kitchen, looking disturbingly refreshed and determined. The scent of alpine air seemed to brand him. Kurt Majors was every inch a male. A determined, impossible male, her mind added.

Thoughts jumbled and tumbled, making the formation of a complete sentence all but impossible. "I thought you were—"

"Gone?" Kurt shook his head. "Told you I intended to stop you from going sperm hunting."

His voice slid through her, the masculine cadence both a promise and a threat.

"By the way, I emptied your suitcase. Coffee?"

"Coffee?" she asked, mentally stumbling as she tried to keep up with his conversation.

"Made a fresh pot."

Fuming, she leaned down to unzip her suitcase. As he'd said, it was empty. "You have no right." She swung around. "This is my life, my choice. Mind your own business."

"Always this cranky before your first cup?"

How was it possible she hadn't heard him moving around? She'd lain in bed, listening for any sound. When she was convinced he was still asleep, or better yet, that he'd left her house, she'd crept from bed and cracked open her bedroom door. The pillows on the couch were strewn haphazardly across the cushions, but there had been no sign of Kurt.

While she had showered, a mixture of emotions had cascaded over her the same way the water did. Time hadn't helped; his rejection still rankled. More, her own foolishness stung. She wasn't normally impulsive and now wished to heaven she hadn't deviated from that routine.

With a sigh, Jessie had pushed away the pain and regret, letting them wash down the drain.

In their place excitement had slowly started to build as realization dawned. Today she was supposed to drive to Denver. With luck, by this time next year she'd have her own child to nurture.

After drying off, she'd dressed in jeans and a white cotton shirt, her insides humming with anticipation.

That lasted until she saw Kurt.

Yesterday she'd seen him as the answer to her prayers. This morning he quite literally stood between her and her dreams.

"Cream and sugar?" he asked.

Telling herself that she could buy clothes in Denver, she grabbed her purse.

"Your car keys are in my pocket."

Her temper flashed. She stalked into the kitchen. Ignoring the fact that he was holding a mug of coffee and paying no attention to the differences in their height and weight, she poked her finger into his chest. "You are the most insufferable, arrogant, male..."

"Yes?"

"...jerk that I have ever met."

"Ouch."

"Get out of my house and my life."

"No can do." He reached down and shoved the cup onto the telephone stand. "Tell you what, I'm willing to make a deal."

Her eyes narrowed, but her breaths continued in shortened gasps of fury. She dropped her hands to her sides, suddenly realizing she was touching him. From the flash in his eyes, she knew he'd noticed, too.

Something was happening to her, something she didn't like, something she couldn't stop.

She had never misbehaved in her life. Now, in seconds, Kurt had pushed past all her inhibitions, uncovering parts of her personality that she hadn't suspected existed. It scared her.

"If you can convince me, in say, five days, that this is a smart thing, that collecting the donation of some man you don't know, a man who could be a rapist or murderer—"

"More likely a med school student—"

"*If* you can convince me this is a good idea, I'll drive you to Denver myself." His voice dropped to a cajoling tenor. "What do you say? Deal?"

"It's not your deal to make."

"Maybe not," he agreed. "But I've got your clothes and your keys."

Her fingernails carved half-moons into her palms. "You're holding me prisoner."

"Offering you a chance to think this through."

"I'll call the sheriff."

"Go ahead. Doesn't matter to me if this is splashed all over the *Courier*."

He was bluffing. He had to be. "It won't be."

"Miss Starr doesn't have contacts?"

Jessie's stomach tightened and frustration clawed at her.

"Five days, Jessie. I'll convince you to do this the right way."

"Your way," she bit out, hardly able to keep her thoughts straight. He'd backed her into a corner, a place she swore she'd never allow herself to be in again.

She'd fought long and hard, surviving the years of being alone and unwanted, helpless to make her own decisions. And she'd nearly thrown away her independence on Sam. Instead she'd learned the lesson, in her heart as well as her mind. Reinforced by pain, it wasn't one she'd soon forget.

"Well?"

"Never," she said.

"That's your final answer?"

"Yes." She'd won. She'd stood up for what she believed, had refused to cower, had proven she was in control of her own life.

"Play it your way."

She exhaled. Now that she'd won, she could afford to be gracious. She knew he cared about her as a friend. Sometimes friends did extreme things. As long as he stayed out of her business from now on, she'd forgive him this once.

Somehow, though, his capitulation seemed easy. Too easy, maybe. "I appreciate your concern. Really I do." In a way, she did.

Since she had no relatives, Mary had become Jessie's confidant. Mary had expressed her reservations about Jessie's decision to become pregnant, but since the first time they'd spoken of it, Mary had resolutely kept her opinions to herself.

Brother and sister had nothing in common, apparently. "Now if you'll give me the keys, please."

"I'd rather we hadn't had to do it this way."

Before she had time to blink, he'd swung her from the floor.

Her breath whooshed out when her stomach connected with his shoulder. She hung upside down, grabbing for his well-worn leather belt, staring at the contours of his buttocks and powerful thighs.

She struggled, wiggling around, but didn't dare move too much for fear of dislodging herself and toppling to the floor. "Kurt!"

"Worked my way through college calf roping," he said, a palm pressed against her spine. "Keep still before I practice those ties on you."

"You can't do this. You said..."

"I said I'd stop you."

He pivoted, and she fought a wave of dizziness. The room spun beneath her.

"Put me down!"

He ignored her.

"You were going to give me five days!"

"I will."

When he opened the front door, winter's last lash stole what little remained of her breath.

"Morning, Mrs. Johnson!" Kurt called out.

Jessie kicked, futilely trying to connect with bone and muscle.

"Morning, Kurt. Jessie."

Jessie groaned, fully convinced she was going to die of mortification now that the neighbors had witnessed this horrible event. She wouldn't die, though, she vowed, until after she killed Kurt.

"Are you two going somewhere?"

"Taking Jessie away for a few days."

"Have a nice time. I'll keep an eye on the house."

He opened the door to his pickup truck and dumped Jessie unceremoniously on the seat. Then he leaned toward her. "Unless you want the neighbors to really enjoy the show, stay right where you are."

She battled the temptation to run, but he was taller, faster and didn't mind making a scene. Jessie didn't want this to be splashed all over the *Courier,* but she doubted he'd mind at all.

"Understand?"

She slumped in her seat, and he slammed the door.

Within seconds, he sat beside her on the unyielding, cold leather. When he looked at her, his eyes were every bit as cold and unyielding.

"You're kidnapping me." Shock dulled her words.

"Yep."

He had her; they both knew it.

A chill chased through her. Question was, what did he intend to do next?

Three

What had she gotten herself into?

Anger and frustration were two sides of the only coin she possessed. No matter which way that coin landed, she didn't have a chance.

Kurt moved around the kitchen, ignoring the impatient tapping of her fingers on the table.

She could call for Columbine Crossing's one taxi, but Kurt would stand in the way of her leaving. If she called Mary, Mary would probably throw her alliance with her brother...after all, Mary hadn't liked Jessie's motherhood idea much better than Kurt did. Even if Jessie called someone from the children's center, Kurt was too well-known and—damn it—respected for anyone to take her seriously.

She fumed. If she didn't get out of here in under an hour, she wouldn't make it to Denver in time.

Irritation gnawed at her. He had no right, was out of his mind. She'd told him that half a dozen times in the truck.

He'd turned up the radio. Garth Brooks singing about a long-neck bottle of beer only drowned out her complaints.

The fact she knew Kurt would never do anything to harm her, that he believed he had her best interests at heart, did nothing to improve her mood. If anything, it made it worse.

Sunshine, Kurt's very pregnant golden retriever, waddled across to Jessie, the dog's toenails clicking on the scarred vinyl flooring. Sunshine placed her head in Jessie's lap. At least it was nice to have one ally.

"Breakfast?"

"Breakfast?" she repeated incredulously.

"Thought you might be hungry."

He was acting so cool and calm, as if something like this happened every day. Maybe to him it did. It didn't to her.

"Being held prisoner killed my appetite."

"Fine."

Agitated, she stood. Sunshine gave a soft whine of protest, but then curled up beneath the table, a paw across her nose, ignoring the humans.

Jessie strode to the sink, her footsteps sounding out her hostility. He didn't react; he just hummed the same Garth Brooks tune that he'd cranked up in the truck.

What was it about men that made them think themselves omniscient?

Sam had been the same way, always knowing what was best for her, even convincing her that making love before marriage was a good idea. After all, he'd said, he wanted to make sure they were compatible before they actually tied the knot.

She pressed her hands to her face.

Agreeing with Sam's suggestion wrapped her dreams in the reality of an unhappily ever after.

When she found a way out of Kurt's reach—and she would, in under an hour—she vowed she would never see him again. He could find someone else to do his book-keeping, find some other woman's life to interfere in. Those thoughts provided the only solace she'd had since he'd pounded on her door last night.

"I'm making eggs."

She remained silent.

Outside, a layer of frost had painted the budding branches on trees...trees that stood as solitary against the elements as she felt against Kurt.

As far as she looked, there wasn't another house in sight. The vista of high mountain prairie stretched before her, boldly spreading out until surrendering at the base of Eagle's Peak.

She'd known Kurt and Mary when their parents had bought their first few acres of land. Now, as sole owner, Kurt had turned it into a thousand. Sheer determination accomplished his goals, Miss Starr had once reported.

Jessie belatedly realized she should have recognized that Kurt's determination would prove to be her undoing.

Was it only last night that Kurt and his home represented hope?

The scent of strong coffee permeated the oversize room. The sound of a satisfying sizzle accompanied the aroma. She turned in time to see him dribble the rest of the whipped eggs into the waiting iron skillet.

Her body betrayed her. Her stomach growled.

Without offering a second time, he poured himself a mug of coffee, taking it straight up, the way one of her foster father's had, with whiskey.

That memory made her shiver.

"Cold?"

From the bones, out. Didn't Kurt miss a thing? "I'm fine. As fine as someone who's been kidnapped can be."

"Good."

She scowled at him, without any effect. He took another drag from the mug, and when the toaster popped up two perfect slices of bread, her stomach growled once more.

Kurt removed a single plate from the cupboard, then pulled a knife and fork from a drawer. "Even a condemned man gets a last meal," he stated. "It's okay to admit defeat."

"You don't know me."

"I intend to."

Their gazes connected. He held it as captive as he'd earlier held her body. In that moment, things crystallized. Kidnapping her hadn't been an impulse. She should have known that. He did things carefully, calculatingly.

To win.

A second shiver, this time nothing to do with a chill, raced through her.

"There's enough for both of us. If you intend to fight me, you need to keep your strength up."

He'd offered her a way out without having to back down. She appreciated that more than words could express. He wasn't an ogre. At least not all of the time. "You cooked, I'll do the dishes."

"Lady, I might never let you go." He set another place at the table and fed a couple more slices of bread into the toaster's waiting slots. "So, Jessie," he said, pouring her an unasked for—but very much needed—cup of coffee. "What are you going to tell your child when he asks about his father?"

Hunger faded. His chivalry had only been an act to catch her off guard. He *was* an ogre.

She slid into a chair, her spine supported by the rigid back. "I was going to decide on that when the time was right."

"How many other things haven't you thought about?

Isn't there a place on the birth certificate for the father's name?''

"Of course.''

"And if I'd agreed to your business arrangement, would you have put my name there?''

She wrapped her hands around the mug he'd placed in front of her, not because she was going to take a drink, but because she needed something to hang on to, something to do.

She should have realized Kurt would show no quarter; he hadn't last night, nor had he given up this morning. Up until three hours ago, she'd thought tenacity was a positive trait.

Time ticked, tension threading between each second.

"Would you have put my name there?'' he repeated very, very quietly.

"No.''

Thunder clouded his eyes, darkening them to stormy forest green. His brow furrowed and a pulse thumped in his temple. She should have lied.

She should have lied.

"And you wanted me to keep quiet about it being my kid? You wanted me to sit back and live in the same town as you and watch you raise our child, my child, *my child,* and pretend nothing happened, that I had no part in it?''

The words were carefully cloaked in a quiet tone that scared her much more than his anger.

At that moment, she saw things clearly from Kurt's point of view. She winced.

She'd always considered herself unselfish—until she was faced with the awful realization that in asking him to help her out, she had been anything but unselfish.

He shoved his untouched plate toward the middle of the table.

She shrunk back.

"Hadn't thought of that, either?"

This time, his question landed with a squeeze around her midsection, like a lasso inexorably being tightened, cutting off her air.

"Why, Jessie?"

She didn't pretend to misunderstand. Kurt wanted answers, deep answers, ones that threatened to bare her soul. And he deserved them.

She doubted she'd done anything more painful in her entire life.

"You were right earlier," she admitted quietly, looking at him and accepting the full force of the hostility he directed toward her. "When you said I was trying to make up for what I didn't have, you were right." Until now, she hadn't been honest with anyone, including herself.

Jessie hoped he'd acknowledge what she'd said and allow both of them to move on. Instead he remained silent, waiting while she exposed the secrets she'd rather keep buried.

"I've never told anyone else this, not even Mary."

He nodded.

Realizing that was all the encouragement he intended to give her, she continued. "I grew up believing in ideals. I wish I still did. I was found on the steps of the church. The doctors thought I was about a week old."

Kurt cursed.

"No one knew where I came from, or when I was born. I've never had a birthday celebration. I don't even know when my real birthday is."

Jessie stared into the inkiness of the cooling black coffee. "I never had my own room, my own clothes, my own family." She paused, the past mingling with the present.

"The only thing I ever truly had of my own was the teddy bear that they found me with."

A newly forming tear prickled the corner of her eye. She wished more than anything, that she could blink it away. "Even that, one of my foster parents took away when I misbehaved."

She looked at Kurt then. The furrow between his brows had eased, but not the anger. She wondered, though, if it was still directed at her. "I wouldn't eat my peas," she said, the distance of years not helping her to make sense of the incident. "And for that, they took away my teddy bear. I cried myself to sleep for three nights. No one cared."

Once more, he swore softly and savagely. Not at her, but for her.

She was discovering that this man—someone she believed she knew completely—possessed depth that she never would have suspected.

"No one should have to experience that."

They both knew how well that kids did all too often. In their volunteer work, they saw the results of not enough time, neglect, hurt.

"It won't happen in my house," she said. It was more than a statement; it was an oath.

"I know."

For that moment, she believed he did. "I want to give my child the love I never felt, the love I never had."

He exhaled. "And two people can give twice the love."

She twisted her lips wryly. "I wish every kid could have the same kind of childhood that you and Mary did. Heaven knows, I dreamed of it enough nights. Believe it or not, Kurt, seeing the love your family had for each other helped me get through the rough spots. It was a wonderful image to hold on to."

"Damn it, Jessie."

"I wasn't jealous, Kurt. It was more like a Cinderella story, something you keep hoping will happen to you."

"Didn't Cinderella find a prince?"

"In real life, the prince is likely to be a frog."

"Like Sam."

She ventured a smile, one that fell before fully forming. She'd gotten over Sam, telling herself he wasn't the right man for her, but the scars lingered.

"That doesn't mean you won't find the right man."

She picked up the mug, nearly sloshing coffee over the rim. Kurt couldn't know how badly she wanted just that, and how much she'd tried to believe that Sam was that man. After all, he'd proposed to her, making her, for three weeks, deliriously happy. Reality intruded all too soon and she learned she truly was an ugly duckling in a world filled with beautiful swans.

Kurt curved his hand over hers, guiding the mug back to the tabletop.

A shock of unwanted awareness reverberated up her arm and skittered across into her heart. His hands were work hardened, rough and masculine. In that moment, they were also protective.

How she longed to surrender to that, buy into the belief that someone other than herself could make everything all right.

She inhaled the crispness of the mountain morning that still clung to him, a scent he alone seemed to own.

He waited with infinite patience. Confound him. This, though, was one truth she couldn't admit, not to him, not to anyone. "I don't want a man."

"Your child will want to know its father."

She closed her eyes, wishing he'd go away, wishing this was all a nightmare.

"What have men ever done that's so bad you've decided that not one of us is worth anything?"

His voice hypnotized her. Low and mellow, it made her want to trust, compelled her to let him dangerously close to discovering what was there, inside her, beneath everything else. "It's more complicated than that."

This Kurt, the man determined to see himself as her savior, was unlike any she'd ever met. The only problem was, she didn't want a savior.

"Tell me."

"If I do..." Jessie chose her words with great care. Her heart thundered as she debated the emotional cost of revealing something she'd shared with no other person. Swallowing, she looked at him and fought to steady her voice. "Will you take me back home so I can get to Denver on time?"

He shook his head. "Can't make that promise."

Defeat dropped on her shoulders like an avalanche devouring everything in its path.

"This is important to you. I understand that." He stood and moved over to the counter, as if needing to distance himself.

"You can't possibly understand."

"Then make me."

She glanced at the clock on the wall behind Kurt. Her stomach knotted with each second that took her further away from her goal.

"What time's your appointment?"

"Noon."

He checked his watch. "Are you going to call them and let them know you're not coming?" He folded his arms across his chest. "Or should I?"

"Neither."

He said nothing. He wanted to reach out, ease the hurt, soothe the ache that she thought only a child could cure.

She hid something from him. He wanted to cut through all the layers, opening them and examining them. Not only that, but he vowed not to rest until he'd accomplished just that, until he won. "Phone's on the stand."

"Forget it, Kurt."

He stood and scraped the uneaten eggs into Sunshine's bowl. She wagged her tail appreciatively as she waddled toward her dish. "I've got chores."

Not looking at her, he pocketed the keys that lay on the counter. They joined her set, the ones he'd taken earlier. No sense offering temptation. Then he grabbed a coat from the peg by the door.

After shrugging into it, he gave a half salute with his index finger. "I'll be back by lunch." His hand closed around the doorknob.

"Wait."

He froze, releasing his grip and turning back toward her. Her face was devoid of all color, pale and drained, made even more stark by the whiteness of her cotton shirt. He wanted to take away the pain on her face, heal it and promise everything would be better. Instead he stayed where he was, giving her space.

He stayed where he was, needing the space himself.

"At one time I believed that a two-parent family was best for a child, just like you do."

"Go on." Kurt could listen to her speak all day. He'd heard her with the kids at the center, the perfect blending of sympathetic and firm. She managed to get them to open up, better than he did. Better than almost anyone, including the center's director.

Now, though, her soft voice was laced with other things, an imploring, intense lilt that slowed his heartbeat by more than a few beats a minute. It made him think of cognac on a cold, clear night.

More than that, it made him long to hold her, fight her battles and slay her dragons.

Some might believe that dragons only existed in the fairy tales. Kurt knew differently. He saw dragons every week, in the expressions and words of the kids he and Jessie worked with. He saw them now, in the curve of her spine, the defeat in her shoulders.

Maybe when this was all over, she'd see things differently, not have kids until she could give them a two-parent family, like his.

"I've always wanted kids. Sam said he'd be willing to go through that once, if I insisted."

Kurt sneered. "If you insisted?"

"That's the way he put it. As if he were doing me a great favor. I guess he didn't want children...said it made women fat and unattractive. And those stretch marks... But he would make the ultimate sacrifice, one time, with the hopes it would produce a boy."

Kurt never much cared for Samuel Bucket, but he'd tolerated him, until the day he'd punched the older boy out, on the school playground. He'd been in second grade, Sam in fourth, if Kurt remembered correctly.

Bucket had shoved Missy Anderson off a swing, then snatched the wooden seat and pushed off with his toes, barely missing Missy's head with his forward motion. When the girl cried, her knees scuffed and her dress torn, Bucket had laughed.

If he had it to do all over again, Kurt would have broken Bucket's nose. "He didn't deserve you."

Cloudiness gusted across her eyes, blue vanquished beneath the somberness of gray. He didn't like it. Didn't like that he caused the pain she couldn't disguise, didn't like the fact he'd forced her into a confession. And was now keeping her away from the only thing she really wanted.

Kurt had to remind himself he liked the idea of her being a single mother even less.

Confession was good for the soul, wasn't it? Suddenly he wondered if it really was.

"Actually I guess I didn't deserve him."

Kurt scowled.

"After…" She pressed her fingers to her temples. "Oh, Lord, I had no idea this would be this difficult."

Patience, not one of Kurt's virtues, strained his control.

She made tiny circles with her fingers, as if fighting a headache. "You have to realize how difficult this is."

"I promise you, Jessie, everything you tell me remains here."

"You know," she said, her motions slowing, then ceasing, "after all this, I shouldn't believe you, but I do."

Long moments passed. He took off his jacket—he hadn't noticed the heat till now—and then, when Jessie spoke again, it was with flatness, the words hollow, devoid of emotion or reaction. He could only guess what the admission cost her, only surmise how much Sam destroyed on his way out.

"Sam called off our engagement when he discovered we were—that is, he said we were sexually incompatible."

Air whooshed out of Kurt's gut with as much heat as a solar flare. He felt sucker-punched. Sick.

"Sonofabitch."

Kurt clenched his fists. Sunshine snarled protectively.

If Kurt ever ran in to Bucket, he'd teach the man a lesson. After what the jerk had done to Jessie, a score needed to be settled. Kurt didn't mind collecting on debts.

"It's okay," she said softly. "I'm over it."

Yeah. Right. If she was over it, she'd have found another

eligible bachelor, gotten married and settled down to raise a family instead of making appointments at a clinic in Denver and asking her friend's brother to provide a sperm donation.

"So that's my deep dark secret." Her voice warbled, shaky with exhalations and honesty. "No man would willingly father my child."

"What the hell does that mean?"

Bright red highlighted her cheekbones. But when she looked at him, the spark of anger had collided with the clouds, resulting in passion, fiery and intriguing. He liked her angry. It was better than dejected.

"Answer me this, Kurt..." She tipped back her chin, looking at him unflinchingly. "Why would any man sleep with me if there was no pleasure in it for him?"

Lord, Jessie's courage astounded Kurt.

Forcing his fingers to unfurl, he plowed them into his hair. Bucket had done a number on her if she actually believed that. Kurt struggled for control, never having had it tested in his life as much as in the past twenty-four hours. Even Belinda, lying, betraying Belinda, hadn't driven him to this deep an emotional level.

He paced the length of the kitchen half a dozen times. Then he stopped, only inches from where Jessie still sat.

He inhaled the scent of her, fresh and crisp, but not from any fancy cologne or perfume. Quite simply, it was unique and undeniably feminine. Why hadn't it ever affected him before?

He took one more step toward her and a pulse leaped in her throat. Unbelievably so did his. "Men and women aren't incompatible, Jessie. Doesn't work that way. Men and women fit together. They're made to form a whole."

"Not if the woman doesn't respond to a man's touch."

The Ice Princess. The words echoed in his mind. Bucket

had called her an Ice Princess. "If a woman doesn't respond to a man's touch, then the man doesn't know how to touch a woman."

Her head dipped then, but not before he caught another glimpse of her features, and the fresh flush that started from her throat and suffused her face.

"What if he doesn't want to touch her?"

"Doesn't want...? Damnation, Jessie, just what the hell are you saying?"

"I'm not... Sam didn't find me attractive enough to keep himself aroused, you know when we were—"

Kurt bit out a word his mother would have washed his mouth out for.

"Kurt!"

Since he wasn't a hypocrite, he figured he wouldn't waste the breath on an apology. "You actually believed that?"

"Sam was the only man who ever got that close to me, and I couldn't keep his interest."

She stood, bringing them closer than comfort allowed.

A response, nothing to do with protecting her, stirred in Kurt's groin.

"So it's easy for you to say that I should find a father for my child, marry him and we could be the perfect family. He asked for his ring back, told me I didn't arouse him and that he'd give his ring to a woman who actually turned him on.

"He said..." She inhaled. "That I was lucky he kissed me."

Even though this had to sting, Jessie didn't run as he half expected. She'd shown more strength in the past day than he'd seen from a woman in the past decade.

"That's why I need to do it this way. No man wants me."

"That's a lie, Jessie."

She drew her lower lip between her teeth. "Even you turned me down last night."

"Woman, you're the most infuriating—" Reaching out, he grabbed her, holding her tight.

She winced.

He didn't relent.

Guilt clawed him, threatening to separate conscience from good judgment. She saw last night as a rejection, proof positive that she was unattractive. Kurt cursed himself. He wasn't known for stupidity...then again, maybe he should be.

Jessie had offered herself to him. He'd sent her home.

Jerk.

She'd been right about that. Jerk was closer to the mark than he cared to admit.

He measured his words and tone, realizing he had little effect on either. "You can't believe I didn't want you last night."

"That's what you said, just like Sam."

"I didn't say I didn't want you, Jess. I said I didn't want to make love just to provide you with a donation." He'd pushed too far to back down now. "Bucket had a problem of his own, one he couldn't face, one he blamed on you."

She shook her head. "You know, at the center, people say that you always know the right words."

"These aren't words, Jessie, they're fact."

"Kurt, I appreciate what you're trying to do—"

"I'm trying to get you to see reality. You are not unattractive."

"So ugly I'm cute?"

"Don't even go there," he warned, the threat rolling with a growl.

She blinked.

"Tell me, Jess, did Bucket kiss you?"

"Of course he did."

"How?"

"How? What do you mean?"

"Tell me about his technique."

"This is ridiculous."

"Humor me."

She took a shaky breath. "Well, on the first date, he kissed me on the back of the hand."

And she'd fallen for the knight in shining armor move. The man was a coward. Had to work his way up to a real kiss.

Kurt would have kissed her hand, too. Eventually. He wouldn't have started there, he would have ended there, after kissing his way from her neck and then down her arm. "Was it a long kiss, Jessie, or just a quick one?"

"A quick one."

He nodded. "And on the second date? The cheek, right?"

"Yes."

"How many dates before he kissed you on the lips?"

"How many...? I don't remember." Color deepened, exposing her embarrassment. "Is this really necessary?"

He nodded. "Take a guess, how many dates until he worked up the guts to try to kiss you?"

"Maybe four."

If he hadn't thought Bucket was a fool before now, this would have signed and sealed it. "How long before he touched you below the neck?"

"Kurt, please. You've made your point."

"Did he touch you below the neck after he gave you the ring?"

"Yes."

"The same night he wanted to take you for a test drive?"

She gasped.

Fury percolated as his body hummed, tightening with the draw of sexual energy. "It wasn't about you, Jessie, it was about Bucket's own inadequacies."

"I have a hard time believing that. He was…" She took in a tiny little breath, not enough to fill a hummingbird's lungs. Then, in a pained rush, she finished, "He said he was, you know…" She looked away. "And then he tried to…"

Tension gripped Kurt, an awareness and a demand.

"No one else has asked me out. If it was all about me, wouldn't someone have asked me out?" She met his gaze. "There was no one before Sam."

He had a flashback, to the night of the prom. Jessie and Mary had bought matching dresses. Jessie's had been put back on the hanger without being worn out of the house.

"There's been no one since. It took me a long time, but I finally faced facts and admitted he was right."

The men of Columbine Crossing needed their heads examined—their eyes at least. "Give it time. You're a desirable woman."

Heaven help him, but Kurt was inventorying just how desirable. The list started with her hair, continued with her eyes and smile, the swell of her breasts, the nip at her waist, the feminine flare of her hips, the length of her legs encased in dark denim, and went all the way to the hidden tips of her painted toenails.

"I might have believed that, before you rejected me, too. I thought you might have wanted to make love to me. I'd just hoped it wasn't out of pity."

He'd thought confession would be good for her soul. He hadn't counted on it stealing a strip from his.

"There's nothing pitying about this," he said, pulling

her onto her toes and inexorably closer to him. "This is because I want to."

It wouldn't be on the hand or on her cheek. It would be on the lips.

And when he was done, there wouldn't be any doubt that Bucket's sexual inadequacies weren't about her.

Kurt owed her that.

But as her breath commingled with his and her lips parted in shock, he knew this was about him, too, about his consuming desires.

He'd given her five days to change his mind. Five days? He hoped he survived that long.

Four

No man had ever held her this way, looked at her with such purposeful intent. "Kurt." Her voice wavered with the weight of her inner emotions.

"Shh."

His hands curved around her shoulders, gently but possessively. Would this have been a prelude, she wondered, of what it would have been like if he'd agreed to father her child and make love with her?

Her eyelids drifted shut, and she was barely able to think when he pulled away and whispered, "Open them, Jessie. I don't want there to be any doubt about what's going on between us."

She didn't want this—she didn't. Telling herself didn't seem to help, though. Her body betrayed her. She responded to his soft order and was rewarded with a smile that made her pulse forget its rhythm.

His eyes captured hers, refusing to let her look away.

Jessie told herself Kurt had something to prove...that this was only an experiment, an attempt to make her feel better about Sam's rejection. But even that rationalization didn't help her respond to her mind's urgent command to move away from him, escape while she still had the chance.

Instead she stayed where she was, and if anything, accepted his unspoken urging and swayed slightly toward him.

The first brush of his lips across hers caused her breath to rush out.

It was light, promising, and it created hunger. She was reminded that she was a woman, a woman with wants and needs, but needs no man would ever willingly want to do something about.

This meant nothing to Kurt...but oh, so much to her.

With gentleness she hadn't known him capable of, he lightly skimmed a second kiss on top of the first.

Before she managed to catch her breath and politely thank him for proving his point, he captured her lower lip with his teeth and gently, as though she were a woman of great inspiration, gently drew it into his mouth.

Her knees sagged. Without his support, she knew her legs wouldn't hold her. She sought his strength, taking what he offered.

The world seemed to spin beneath his masterful combination of warmth and moisture.

He tasted of power; she couldn't resist him if she tried. Absently she realized she was no longer making the effort....

His tongue traced her lip, demanding something, something she didn't know how to define. Then his tongue met hers.

Fiery sensations turned molten and flowed through her. Her groan was buried somewhere between them, but then

Kurt blended it back into the kiss. Then he brought one of his hands across her shoulder blade and up the side of her neck, cradling her nape and easing her even closer.

She knew she should react, but didn't know how.

Her breasts brushed his shirt, and even she felt their response as they became heavier and their tips tightened. She'd never experienced these sensations.

Kurt's fingers tangled in her hair and he drew her head back, granting himself further access. Hopelessly falling...falling, she reached up, wrapping her arms around his neck.

In that instant, he shifted their positions, bringing his thigh between her legs. Drawn, as if against her will, she leaned into him, accepting his offer and feeling even stranger sensations building inside, a hunger in a place she didn't know could feel hunger.

Impossibly he deepened the kiss, drawing her into him and making her want only more. Then, in a dance where she didn't begin to understand the steps, he retreated. Loss collided with desire—she didn't want it to end, never wanted it to end.

Still holding her close, he moved his other hand down her back to rest at the base of her spine. The touch thrilled, but it wasn't enough.

She didn't know how to ask for what she wanted, didn't dare. Yet the absence, the need drove her onward.

Boldly, in a way she would have never believed herself capable of, she followed the lead he'd blazed, tentatively touching the tip of his tongue with hers.

Kurt groaned, the sound matching her earlier one. Triumph flashed inside her, a feminine victory scored at the hands of her teacher. Suddenly seeking, she surrendered to her body's instincts, no longer shy, no longer fighting what she couldn't deny.

Within seconds, he took back the initiative, circling and testing, and finally all too soon, ended the kiss.

She blinked uncertainly, not knowing what to say or how to act. Jessie wished she had an air of sophistication that would enable her to be blasé, make an offhanded comment and pretend nothing had happened.

Her breaths came too quickly for that, though, and she felt the thunder of her pulse in her throat. As if reading her thoughts, his gaze went there, noticing the way it pounded.

He already knew no man had kissed her like that, surely he wouldn't take her reaction for anything more than it was. But just what that was, she had no idea.

He eased his hand from her nape, the drag of his work-weary skin abrading her neck, the curve of her cheek, then upward, across the outer, sensitive shell of her ear. His fingers splayed in her hair, feathering the strands back, away from her face.

"Bucket was a fool."

Looking away, she swallowed. His words were a reminder that this had been an experiment. Unfortunately, with the little twist in her heart, she didn't know whether it had failed or whether it had been a huge success. The only thing she knew was that she'd never be the same again.

She'd had a taste of passion and she feared it wouldn't be enough. It would have to be, though. Something as wonderful as this would never happen to her again.

Gently he moved his hand and captured her chin between his thumb and forefinger, exerting just enough pressure to force her to look at him.

His eyes were a darker shade of green than they had been earlier, smoldering with the intensity of a smoky forest fire. "Make the telephone call, Jessie. Or I'll make it for you."

She shuddered.

Make the call?

Not only had he been trying to make a point, but he'd also used the response he'd coaxed against her, trying to bend her to his will. Tears welled and she dashed them away, determined that he not see how he'd affected her.

"Which will it be?"

Frowning, confused and angry, she reached up and pushed his hand away. What was wrong with her? She should have resisted, should never have allowed herself to surrender to Kurt's all-too-real masculinity.

She looked at him, finding his eyes dark and unreadable. The expression she'd seen moments ago had vanished, leaving her to wonder if what she'd read had only been a figment of her desire-sharpened imagination. She wanted to see that the kiss had meant something to him, as much as it had to her.

Obviously it hadn't.

Berating herself for being every kind of fool, she brushed her unruly hair—hair he'd mussed into tangles—back from her face. She knew she didn't inspire passion in men. For a second, though, she'd almost been able to believe...

Determinedly she banished that thought to the back of her heart, where she could take it out and remember it, another time, when hurt didn't overwhelm her.

"Jessie..."

She turned away and crossed to the window, unable to face him any longer. Embarrassment replaced all her other emotions, and she gratefully let it. At least she knew how to function that way. She'd had plenty of experience.

Instead of leaving her alone to her misery, he prompted, "The phone number, Jessie?"

Frustration flared. "Will that get you to leave me alone?"

"For now."

He'd won.

He'd taken the only thing that truly belonged to her, her feelings, and turned them back on her, kissing her until she couldn't think, proving he held the power.

Looking across at the high prairie vista, she offered thanks that he hadn't agreed to her proposal. Heaven only knew what Kurt would have demanded from her if she had to deal with him on a different, more intimate level. His refusal had been a blessing. "I'll call them. And then you can take me home."

Nothingness yawned and stretched.

Finally she turned to face him.

His arms where folded across his chest, legs spread battle-ready wide. "We've been over this before. You're not going anywhere until I have your word that you're admitting defeat."

Even though she should, she couldn't.

"Phone's over there," he said, pointing.

To reach the phone, she had no choice but to pass him. Maybe he'd do the gentlemanly thing and step aside.

Luck wasn't with her. On her way by, her shoulder brushed his arm. He reached out, grabbed her wrist and tugged her to a stop.

"Bucket was a fool," he reiterated.

"Of course he was." Not for a moment did she believe Kurt.

When she pulled away, she realized his touch had seared her indelibly.

Jessie had the number memorized and dialed it shakily. As the ring echoed in her ear, she cradled the receiver with both hands.

The echo of his boots on the hardwood living-room floor told her she wasn't alone. Before she'd heard him, she'd sensed him, every fiber of her being filling with unwelcome anticipation.

The friendly receptionist answered and Jessie looked anywhere but at Kurt. "This is Jessica Stephens," she said, her voice wobbly. "I'd like to…"

Kurt shifted, his boot heel scraping the floor.

She swallowed. "Reschedule today's appointment."

"Reschedule?" Kurt demanded.

"For next week," she told the receptionist.

He moved closer. Even though she didn't see his scowl, she felt its effects, and she rippled with unease.

"Yes, next Wednesday at one is perfect. Thank you." Jessie wondered why the win didn't feel like a victory.

With great reluctance, she hung up. Having wasted as much time as possible, she faced Kurt.

"Next Wednesday?"

She tipped back her head and blinked, smiling falsely as she refused to let him see her uncertainty.

"Why, Jessie?"

She asked herself the same question. If she'd canceled and told Kurt she'd changed her mind, she could escape. She could be at home, away from him, in less than an hour.

But the very act would be a betrayal of everything that drove her. She couldn't do that, not even to save herself.

Without a word, he pivoted. His steps thundered, then diminished with each passing second. The back door slammed, and she jumped.

With him gone, a breath rushed out from somewhere deep inside. She sank onto the couch. Her act of defiance combined with the lingering sensual swirl, leaving her unable to stand.

How had her world become so topsy-turvy?

Yesterday, she'd had an appointment at a clinic, her future was bright and her dreams were falling into place. Now... She'd been rejected, kidnapped and kissed.

She exhaled a shaky lungful of air. The taste of him tantalized her tongue. Her shoulders and wrist tingled where he'd touched, and the scent of his determination surrounded her.

Sunshine meandered over and lay at Jessie's feet. Stroking the dog's nose, Jessie worried about what would happen next, when Kurt returned.

Kurt saddled up and headed for the west side of his property. He'd been meaning to ride the fences for a long time. Today was a better day than others had been. He told himself it was because spring was on its final approach and that the ground was no longer as frozen as it had been a month ago.

But those reasons had only been excuses to get away.

Over the past couple of hours, low-lying clouds had rolled off the mountains, hanging over the land, thick with threat. The sun had been obscured, not even a single ray made its way through the soupy gray. Suited him fine. The sky matched his mood.

Tension churned in his gut. And no matter how fast he rode, he couldn't escape the regret chasing him.

Just what in the hell did he think he was doing?

Kissing Jessie had been a mistake. She was fragile and hopeful, a lethal combination. But that hadn't stopped him from plowing right into the middle of her emotions and tying his up with them.

As the wind gusted, icy tentacles of winter's final attempt to grip the earth stabbed his exposed skin. He welcomed it as a way to banish thoughts of her, the remembrance of her.

It didn't work.

He recalled the way she'd looked at him, blue eyes wide and expressive, like a columbine turned trustingly toward the sun. She hadn't wanted to believe him. Obviously she had good instincts. He'd intended to prove Bucket was a fool. But Kurt had succeeded in proving himself a bigger one.

Bucket may not have had a reaction to her. Kurt sure as hell had.

He never expected it, never wanted it. He had no intention of ever caring for a woman again, not since Belinda slept with one of his ranch hands. Since then, Kurt embarked on a few meaningless relationships, casual dates and occasional dances at the Wooden Nickel Saloon. But his experience that morning with Jessie was different.

When he'd brushed his lips across hers, he'd thirsted for more. The second kiss should have been enough to show her she was responsive, but it wasn't. He'd taken it further, touched his tongue to hers.

In that instant, something changed. A deep part of him, one that was destroyed by his ex-wife, started to open up. Want turned into pain, diluting it.

His masculine urges had taken over, and Kurt wanted Jessie to desire him. He'd backed off, encouraging her to come to him, moving his leg between her thighs and drawing her closer. Instead of proving she wasn't cold, he'd proven he was hot.

That wasn't part of the bargain.

When he asked her to call the clinic, he'd seen confusion in her eyes, with hurt trumping the yearning that had just been there. Kurt didn't know when he'd become a bastard. Problem was, he hadn't known what to do about his reaction.

Kurt realized that if he had half a brain, he'd take her home, forget about her outrageous proposal, allow her to make her own mistakes. Her determination to become a mother wasn't his problem. Frankly it wasn't even his business. He knew all that. Rationally.

Unfortunately he didn't even have half a brain where she was concerned.

In coming to him, she'd involved him. His code of ethics didn't allow him to turn his back, even though he wanted to do just that. Until now, he'd learned to trust his instincts. With her, he was closing the door without looking back.

He swallowed, but the taste of her—temptation and trust—remained on his tongue, walloping him in the solar plexus. He'd never been with a more sweetly sensual woman.

There was no other woman like Jessie. And he'd never experienced such raw longing before. That bothered him more than anything.

He'd always been able to hold back, control his desire. That had been something else that had driven Belinda to take another man into Kurt's bed—she'd wanted a man who would lose himself in her. He never had.

But with Jessie... The honesty of her response had pushed him past reason.

It couldn't happen again, for her sake and especially for his.

Kurt took longer than he needed to ride the fence line, restringing barbed wire and pounding fence posts into the reluctant ground.

By late afternoon, dusk devoured opaque clouds. He'd missed lunch and he acknowledged he was stalling. Tipping back the brim of the battered Stetson, he mounted Lasso, his horse, and turned toward the ranch house.

By the time he'd groomed and fed the stallion, the sun's final salute skirted the nearby mountain peaks. Kurt figured he'd killed another hour. That left him just four and a half more days to get through.

He entered through the back door. Sunshine thumped her tail, but she didn't bound over to greet him. Crossing the floor, Kurt crouched next to the retriever, scratching behind her ears. "Won't be long, girl," he promised. She looked at him through dark, tired eyes, as if holding him to his promise.

"When are her puppies due?"

He glanced up. Jessie stood there, looking down at him, her hair falling forward to curtain her face. He recalled the way his fingers had explored the silkiness earlier. He itched to do it again, but this time, he'd draw the strands across his lips.

"Kurt?"

What the hell had she asked him?

"The puppies?" she reminded him. "When are they due?"

He cleared his throat. "Any day."

"Maybe I'll still be..." She didn't finish.

"Yeah, maybe you will be," he said. Unless she conceded the battle, she wasn't going anywhere soon.

He stood, bringing them closer together. She took a step back. The atmosphere had suddenly changed. In that instant, camaraderie had vanished.

Kurt looked at her, focusing on her lips, then on her eyes. Tension tightened around them. He saw it in the way her chest rose with a deep breath, felt it in the way his stomach constricted.

"Dinner?" she asked, the word a single rush.

He raised a brow.

"It's late, and you haven't eaten since breakfast. At least, I assume you haven't. I thought you might want a steak or..."

He waited.

"Or something," she finished saying.

His body voted for "or something."

"You offering?"

"You cooked breakfast."

Kurt had no idea how long it had been since a woman had made him a meal. He liked the thought of it, liked the thought of having company during the long, cool night.

Until he'd walked in the door five minutes ago, he hadn't realized how much he missed companionship. There was something about the scent of a woman, the sound of her voice. Not just any woman—Jessie—with soft perfume and a softer tone.

"I found steaks in the freezer...I already defrosted two. I hope that's okay."

"I'll wash up, then give you a hand."

Kurt noticed that she didn't move until after he did. Probably better that way. He doubted he would have been able to resist the impulse of touching her.

She moved farther into the kitchen. Sunshine roused herself and followed Jessie. So, not even man's most loyal friend was immune. He told himself it was the steaks; he knew better.

He headed upstairs toward the master bedroom, noticing, for the first time since he'd thrown Belinda out, how sterile the room seemed.

No pictures graced the walls, no pillows scattered across the bed, no knickknacks adorned the dresser...unlike Jessie's bedroom. He'd glimpsed her bedroom this morning, shamelessly looking in while she showered. With comforters and cushions, the room had been inviting, encouraging him to enter and stay.

He hadn't.

But the contrast to his own stark life etched sharply in his mind.

His bathroom wasn't much different. His shower had a bottle of combination shampoo and conditioner, along with a single bar of soap. No candles there, or nice smelling packets of something—he couldn't remember what they were called—lining the closet shelves and no squeeze bottles of scented shower gels.

But Kurt hadn't missed having a woman in his life; in fact he preferred it that way. He answered to himself, ate what he wanted, when he wanted, slept when he was tired and had total control of the remote control.

So why did he hurry through his shower in order to get back to the kitchen, to her?

Sunshine thumped her tail, looking up, but not moving. Jessie stood near the window, peeling a potato and humming, off-key. For the first time in two days, he smiled.

Leaning against the door frame, Kurt watched her in silence. He liked the sight of her in his kitchen. His libido supplied an image of another place he'd like to see her.

He shifted and Sunshine looked up, giving a welcoming whine.

Jessie spun, dropping the knife on the floor. Her mouth formed a small circle of kissable shock and his insides tightened.

It would have been better if he hadn't kissed her earlier. That way he wouldn't have known what he was missing. Now he did.

"I didn't hear you come in."

"Because you were humming too loud." Off-key, too.

"I wasn't."

He pushed away from the wall, closed the distance and bent to retrieve the knife. Instead of handing it to her, he dropped it in the sink.

Her nostrils flared slightly, betraying something he knew she was hoping he couldn't read.

Yeah, kissing her had been a thousand acre mistake.

"The steaks need to be put on the grill in a few minutes."

Needing something to do with his hands, he seized the escape. "I'll light it."

"Guess it's true what I heard," she said.

He paused and raised a questioning brow.

"That men will cook if there's danger involved."

"Seem to thrive on danger." Especially him. Instead of grabbing the spatula, he stroked his thumb up the column of her neck. It was dangerous all right.

She caught his wrist, her small hand not reaching all the way around it. "Don't. You've already proven your point."

He frowned. "What point?"

"That you can make me want you."

"If you think that's what—"

"I don't need your pity. I don't want it."

"Pity?" he echoed. "What in the name of creation makes you think any of this has to do with pity?"

She tried to escape his gaze. Pushing aside his hand and pulling away her own, she turned toward the counter.

Kurt was having none of it. Grabbing her shoulders, he forced her to face him.

"Look, Kurt, I know you don't find me attractive, and I know that I couldn't light a fire in a man, even if I had a match."

He stopped short of showing her just how much he was like kindling.

"It's kind of you to—"

"Kind?" The word was bitten into the tension. "There was nothing kind about kissing you and there sure as sunshine wasn't anything pitying about it."

She swallowed. Unflinchingly she met his gaze. He saw disbelief there. How could she possibly believe, after the intensity of their kiss, that it was about anything other than passion, the reaction of a man for a desirable woman?

"Turn off the stove."

She blinked.

"Now."

"Why?" she asked, placing a hand near her throat.

Hoping to still the pounding there? he wondered. He'd seen the leap of her pulse and took encouragement from it. Maybe now she'd believe...

"Turn it off, Jessie."

Slowly she lowered her hand and followed his order. Then, gazing up at him, she dropped her hand to her side. In a single, swift motion, he manacled her wrist.

"What are you doing?"

"Come with me, Jessie."

"Kurt, I..."

He quirked a brow.

"You're scaring me."

"Jessie, you've got two choices. Come willingly..."

She squeezed her eyes shut. "You're giving me no choice again."

"What'll it be?"

"Do you always have to win?"

"Only when it matters."

He grabbed her wrist and she jumped. He felt the frantic drumming of her heartbeat. Absently he brushed his thumb across the thrum. "Come with me, Jessie."

Instead of waiting for her surrender, he tugged her, pulling her toward him.

"Where are we going?"

"To my bedroom."

"Kurt, no!"

Sunshine whined, placing a paw across her eyes.

"Trust me, Jessie." Even as he said the words, he wondered whether he deserved what they implied. When he was finished with her, the word "pity" would no longer be in her vocabulary. "Trust me."

Five

Trust him?

Trust him, how? It would be easier to ride a horse naked through a snowstorm than to give him what he demanded. She didn't know how to give him what he wanted, wasn't sure she even knew how to trust anymore.

"I won't do anything you're uncomfortable with," he promised, his voice drizzling over her in reassuring tones.

That didn't stop nervousness from making her heart thunder in triple time.

His verdant eyes darkening, he asked her to believe in him. Didn't he realize that after all she'd been through, trust was the one thing she could never willingly give him? "I'm…"

He waited. He tightened his hand on her wrist, as if he hoped to telegraph some of his strength into her. It didn't work. Asking him to father her child, combined with her confession that she couldn't interest a man, had drained the last of her courage.

Silence shivered, yet she couldn't complete her sentence.

After a few tense moments, he quietly prompted, "Tell me, Jessie. Talk to me."

She swallowed, trying to find her voice. "I'm uncomfortable with this...with everything."

"Like you were when Bucket tried to seduce you?"

A furious burst of color flashed up her neck, settling on her face. Why did he do this to her? Hadn't she suffered enough humiliation from Sam, without Kurt continuing to remind her of the embarrassment?

She turned her head away from him, unwilling to see his sympathy.

"That was inexcusable. Jessie, I'm sorry. I shouldn't have said that."

But just like Sam he had said things that still echoed in her mind. "Just let me go. Let go of my hand. Let me go home."

He didn't answer. Then, with his free hand on her chin, he gently turned her head so that she looked at him again. A callused fingertip grazed her cheek, as if he was highlighting the flush painted in them.

"I can't let you go, Jess."

"Can't?" she asked. "Or won't?"

"Won't."

Her lips parted and air rushed through them.

Kurt exerted more pressure on her wrist, his warmth clashing with the goose bumps raised on her arms.

"I'm not going to seduce you."

Her insides leaped at his words, the hint of intimacy. Then she told herself that of course he wouldn't seduce her. He wasn't willing to make love with her. She knew that. Still, her mind supplied all-too real images of what it might be like, and that was enough to make her mouth dry.

"Upstairs," he said.

She gasped, unable to believe his arrogance after she'd told him she was uncomfortable with the whole thing. "Kurt..."

"Okay, Jessie, it's my way or my way. Three seconds before I decide for you."

He would, too. She knew it. Kurt obviously wasn't satisfied with the point he'd proved earlier when he kissed her. He wouldn't be happy until she was completely mortified.

Closing her eyes, she offered a prayer for survival—not only that, but for escape, too.

"One."

She opened her eyes again. His brows were set in a formidable line above determined green eyes. He intended to win. That left her as the loser.

"Two."

"Don't do this to me."

"Three."

He was serious.

Bending, he lifted her from the floor. "In my arms or over my shoulder?" He cradled her tightly against his chest, her head nearly resting on his shoulder. "Your choice."

"Wait." She could barely think, let alone talk. This morning, when she'd been upside down, her hair trailing down the back of his cotton shirt and her hand desperately hanging onto his belt, sensations she'd thought never to experience had shimmied through her, leaving her dizzy. "I'll come willingly."

He buried his flash of triumph beneath a quick nod.

Her feet brushed the floor once, twice, before he finally

let her go. She was tired of his caveman act and a part of her rebelled against it, and yet... And yet a secret, suppressed part of her relished being the center of his attention. If she wasn't careful, she could get used to it.

Her own reactions bothered her more than anything he might do to her.

Drawing her toward the stairs, he turned on the lights. Sunshine lifted her head, then lazily dropped it back down again. Jessie wished the dog would follow them, anything to provide a buffer between her and Kurt and whatever was happening deep inside her.

At the top of the stairs, Jessie's steps faltered. Her heart pounded and her instinct warned of danger. She'd never been inside a man's bedroom before.

Kurt kept up the pressure around her wrist. She would have run, otherwise. Maybe he knew that; maybe he just wasn't taking any chances.

With his foot, he opened the door, leaving the room dark, depriving her of sight even though he instinctively moved across the floor, the sound of his boots against the floor and her senses.

"Close your eyes."

"It doesn't matter," she said shakily, wondering if that was truly her voice trembling in the night. "I can't see anything."

"Close them anyway."

This total trust terrified her more than the idea of spending the rest of her life alone.

In his hands, he held the potential to humiliate her beyond anything she'd ever known.

"Jessie?" His voice reverberated in the stillness, shrouded by lightning and spring rain.

"I don't know if I can do this," she confessed.

"You've known me for years, Jessie. Have I ever hurt you before?"

Until yesterday, she hadn't asked him to father her baby.

"Jess?" he demanded urgently.

"Okay," she said. "I closed them."

"Good."

A few seconds later, he released her. Now she strangely longed for the lifeline of his touch.

Deprived of sight, her other senses seeped in to fill the void. His scent swirled around her, and she inhaled it with every breath. His boots scraped once, twice, then again as he moved away.

Her hands curled into tiny balls, her nails biting into her palms. No man had ever asked what he demanded.

An almost silent flick was followed by a shift in brightness. He'd obviously turned on the light, but he stood there, not moving. Looking at her?

Her breaths labored and she struggled to ward off the need to open her eyes. Did he have any idea what he had done to her? He'd made her so very, very aware of what being female meant to an incredibly masculine male.

Sam hadn't been half the man Kurt was. Unfortunately she suspected Kurt knew it, too.

He had power, and with her agreement to come willingly, she'd granted him the right to use it.

She'd forgotten to breathe, but her breath whooshed out when his hand landed on her shoulder.

"Okay," he softly instructed, the word sighing across her ear. "Open your eyes."

She blinked, adjusting from total darkness to bright light. When she focused, she realized she stood in front of a cheval mirror. She blinked, then looked questioningly over her shoulder at Kurt.

"I want you to look straight ahead."

"At what?"

"At yourself."

She frowned. "Have you lost your mind?"

"I know exactly what I'm doing."

Gently he curved his palm against her cheekbone, cradling her face for a second. Without conscious thought, she allowed her eyes to drift shut again. She'd dreamed of being loved, and more, cherished...dreamed a man would hold her tenderly and tell her he cared.

"Tell me what you see."

Fantasy shattered into slivers of reality.

"In the mirror, Jessie, tell me what you see."

He turned her head so that she faced the mirror. Trying to concentrate, she said, "I see you and me." He stood at least half a foot taller than she did. His large hand still rested on her face, and she drew a strange sense of comfort from it.

"Beyond that," he said.

The patter of freezing rain splashed against the window, and darkened shadows cast shifting shapes across the wall. "I don't understand what you're asking me."

"Describe yourself to me."

Confronted with all her obvious flaws, she swallowed deeply. It was enough to know her faults; after all, she saw them in the mirror every morning. But to catalog them for Kurt? She couldn't.

Suddenly desperate to escape, she took a step back, bringing their bodies in contact. Then she froze.

In the glass, she saw his nostrils pinch as he sucked in a sharp breath. Jessie's chest rose and fell in frantic motions, and her thoughts twirled with confusion.

Kurt backed off a few inches, and she remained rooted to the spot.

This was a mistake, a huge one. She shouldn't have

trusted, shouldn't have...but then, in the mirror, their gazes locked.

"It's okay," he said.

Okay for whom? she wondered frantically. He was used to this, having women in his room, having them go along with his daring suggestions, but she was different. Until this morning in his kitchen, she'd never even been properly kissed. There was little doubt that she was no femme fatale.

And the very real throbbing sensation inside her demanded attention, attention she didn't know how to give.

"Keep looking in the mirror," he urged, his voice husky, as if denim had been dragged across barbed wire. "What's the first thing you see?"

Needing to focus, she kept looking at him. "Eyes."

"What color?"

His were green. She'd noticed that before, but until now, she'd never noticed the spikes of gold or the way dark pupils narrowed with intensity. Why hadn't she noticed how very compelling he was before? And for heaven's sake, why was she noticing now?

"What color are your eyes, Jessie?" he asked.

"Blue."

"What color blue?"

She looked again, frowning, but still didn't know how to answer. "Blue-blue."

"Columbine blue," he stated.

"Like the state flower?"

He nodded.

"You're joking."

"No."

She didn't see it. No matter which way she cocked her head, she saw only blue.

"Expressive, moody, hopeful. They reveal what you're thinking, Jessie, telling the secrets you try to keep hidden."

She was afraid to ask, but the question slipped out, as if by its own will. "Like?"

"Like the fact you want to believe what I'm saying, but you're afraid to."

"You see all that?"

"Yeah."

And what else did he see? Did he see how his words were affecting her? Had he seen—even for a moment—the way she'd been fool enough to succumb to her long lost dreams and believe she was all the things she wanted to be?

Terror started as a small tremor in her midsection. Then he halted it with his next question, "What about your ears?"

She couldn't be more off balance if a storm front blew down from Eagle's Peak and knocked her from her feet.

Reaching forward, he brushed back her hair. His fingers skimmed her skin, and until that instant, she hadn't known the flesh of her ear could be so sensitive.

"Turn your head, an inch to the left."

Curious, unable to resist, she did as he asked.

"Now?" he asked, leaning down a bit to whisper into her ear.

His fingers played softly across her. She shivered despite being overly warm. "It's, er, ah, pierced."

"So it is."

She would surely go insane. Right now, however, there wasn't a single place she'd rather go.

"What else?"

"Kurt, I don't know what you want from me."

"Honesty. Nothing less. Is your ear oversize? Does it stick out too far?"

She shook her head.

"Nice ear?" he asked.

"It's an ear." And if he didn't stop soon, she feared she'd beg him never to.

"Hair?"

"Too straight. It needs a curling iron. And it needs trimming." She looked deeper. "Maybe I'll highlight it this summer."

Quietly Kurt said, "Ah, but I can do this..." He wrapped his hand in the blond length, letting it drape across his wrist, then he wound it between his fingers, easing closer and closer to her.

He lowered his head, drawing her hair close to his nose, then inhaling.

Her gulp echoed in her own ears.

"Smells nice," he said. "Fresh. And the length is perfect. It reaches your shoulders. Seems perfect to me."

She shook her head. That succeeded only in bringing them closer together. Her bottom wiggled against him, and she felt him against her, hard.

Jessie froze.

What was happening here? She was out of her comfort zone, way beyond her level of experience.

Lightning sizzled and thunder clapped; she jumped, then regretted it.

Kurt had set out to prove something to her, but what it was, she was no longer sure. She knew she had to get out of here, escape him and his magic, before it was too late, before she truly embarrassed herself.

But he still held her. She dared not breathe, let alone move. Against her back, he was hard. *That much* she understood.

Slowly he unwound the strands of hair from his hand, his fingertips glancing off her throat. She wondered if he felt the pulse frantically thumping there.

"Tell me about your lips," he said quietly, not moving her away, not stepping back himself.

His right hand rested on her shoulder, an odd mixture of possession, demand and comfort.

She didn't want to do this anymore, she wanted safety. But Kurt wasn't ready to relent. "My lips are too thin."

"You have no trouble inventorying your faults."

Neither had Sam.

"I don't want to know about your faults."

His gaze met hers in the mirror She focused, almost desperately, on it.

"Tell me something good," he urged.

"I've never..."

"Thought of yourself that way before?" he asked, a brow raised and his voice soft, blending with the soothing backdrop of rain. "It's time you did, Jessie." With the blunted tip of his thumbnail, he abraded her lower lip.

A warm feeling flooded her insides.

She wanted...she needed...him.

Confusion overrode all other emotions. She knew she wasn't responsive sexually, so what was the empty yearning she felt? She'd always identified it as a need to love and be loved in return, but now...now, she didn't know.

"They smile, a lot," Kurt said when she didn't respond.

With her gaze trained on the mirror, she watched in fascination as he opened the top button of her blouse, peeling back the fabric to expose the hollow of her neck.

She should stop him...

The second button surrendered, as it had last night. But that was where the similarities ended. This time, she watched in fascination as he revealed her chest.

She saw the way he undid the third, noticed the color of his sun-bronzed skin against hers, white from never being exposed.

He watched her in the mirror, watching each of her re-actions as he followed the contours of her bra, his fingernail scraping the front clasp that hid her from him.

Dampness pooled deep in her.

There was no way she'd let him strip her. No way. Never...

The clasp opened.

Her breasts spilled forward, their tips rubbing against her shirt. She groaned.

Looking in the mirror, not down at her, Kurt reached inside her shirt and took the weight of her breasts in his palms.

"Perfect."

Her legs threatened to become rubber.

His calluses scraped her and she cried out.

He'd left her covered with fabric and some sense of modesty, even as she shamefully pressed her nipples against him, seeking more.

He didn't disappoint.

With his thumb and forefinger, he circled her breast, then squeezed gently.

Light flashed in her eyes. She had no idea whether it was lightning or whether it came from inside her. All she knew was that something was devouring her.

"There's so much about you," he said, removing his hands, "that makes a man glad to be a man."

In wide-eyed shock, she turned.

Kurt reacted instantly, capturing her shoulders, holding her in place, drawing her shirt together before he suc-cumbed to the temptation of tasting what he'd felt.

This was wrong, he knew it. He'd given his word. And in less time than the thunderheads collided, he'd nearly broken his vow. "Stay still," he warned, *before I give in and show you just how glad I am to be a man.*

His gut was knotted tighter than a rope around a trussed up calf. Trouble was, he felt as if he'd been trussed, and damn it all if he hadn't thrown the lasso himself.

"Kurt?"

"It isn't ice in your veins, Jessie," he said, looking anywhere but where her cotton shirt gaped. "It's passion, white-hot passion. Bucket didn't know what the hell to do with you."

She blinked and he read the disbelief in her eyes, combined with an almost desperate wish.

"But—"

"Do me a favor. Think long and hard about whether you really want to go to a clinic."

She drew her lower lip into her mouth. That meant it was getting moist.

Hell.

"It's time you went to bed." His voice grated with raw hunger. He needed her out of his room and fast. "Guest room's next door. Make yourself comfortable." It hadn't helped that the mirror showed his reflection, her reflection and the bed's. When she'd innocently wriggled against him, igniting a response, he'd pictured the bed, with them in it.

He'd brought her up here to his room in order to prove a point, not get lost in the process. Right now, he stood in danger of doing exactly that. If he became any more aroused, he may not be responsible for his actions.

That scared the devil out of him. He'd never been past the point of no return with a woman, had always able to hold back. But brushing his thumb across her lip had left him ravenous for more than just a taste.

What in a month of Sundays was wrong with him? He'd intended to show her she was desirable, help her find the confidence she needed to start accepting dates and find love. He hadn't planned on nearly bedding her himself.

He took a step away from her, then turned away. How was it that, until yesterday, he'd had no idea how desirable and exciting she truly was?

He'd worked with her at the center for years; they'd been friends longer than that. Even when she'd been in his house, bent over his books, explaining something to him, he'd seen her as a woman, sure, but noticed nothing beyond the ordinary.

He must have been blind.

Now he wasn't. "Good night," he said by way of dismissal.

"Night," she responded, her words a sensual husk that slid over him, making him think of a down comforter for two, on a long, cold Colorado night.

At the door, she paused, looking back at him. "I don't have any pajamas."

The knot in his gut tightened. Served him right, with his bright ideas. "Here." Going to his closet, he grabbed the first flannel shirt his hand closed around.

He offered it to her. For a moment, she hesitated, giving his imagination enough time to supply the details of what it might look like on her. The soft fabric would skim her thighs and cover her behind...maybe.

The recollection of her pressed against him forced him to stifle a groan.

She accepted the shirt, making sure she never touched him. He gave big thanks for small mercies.

Without a word, she left, her footsteps sounding lightly in the hallway. With more force than necessary, he shut the door, wood bouncing off wood.

She was gone and maybe he'd be able to control the hardness thrusting against his too-damn-tight jeans.

Crossing to the window, he rested his palm on the cold pane. Even there, he couldn't escape her. The overhead light caused the window to become reflective. He saw not only the outline of the mirror, but he saw the lonely double bed.

His hand closed into a fist.

Jessie's scent lingered in the air, a temptation to taunt him. When he'd raised her hair to his face, trailing silk across his chin and inhaling her scent, he'd pictured her hair fanning across his chest. They'd been in the bed, with her propped on an elbow, looking at him. Strands had teased his chest, mingling with the hair there, making him ready...again.

Before he'd brought her to his room, Kurt had promised Jessie he wouldn't seduce her. Then, he'd had no idea how difficult the promise would be to keep.

His body hadn't been so insistent in years. His arms ached to hold her, his mouth wanted another taste of her sweetness. He'd called on reserves he didn't know he had to hold back.

Simply put, he knew that if he'd started to undress her—continued slipping buttons through their holes, and ending with the eventual drag of her jeans zipper—she wouldn't have stopped him.

Jessie wanted a baby, nothing more. If he could supply the donation, all the better. She didn't need him, he reminded himself, all she needed was sperm.

He scowled, the window glaring the intimidating image right back at him.

He'd never wanted a woman as badly as he wanted Jessie. And he'd never wanted not to want a woman as badly as he wanted not to want her.

The muted sound of movement somehow drifted through the walls as Jessie took him up on his offer. He heard the bed squeaking. The sound was too suggestive. Just how comfortable, he wondered, did she intend to make herself?

In frustration, he rapped his knuckles on the glass. For every bit of her comfort, he'd experienced an equal amount of discomfort.

It promised to be a long, long night. Kurt reached for his belt buckle, then realized it wasn't just tonight he was worried about—it was the next five days.

The sound of leather cracked through the stillness as he whipped his belt out of its loops. When had he become the fool Belinda accused him of being?

He had no business becoming aroused by Jessie, even less business contemplating the possibility of going to her now...

Jessie perched on the edge of the bed, then forced herself to move backward, wrapping her arms around her legs. Kurt's shirt draped across the down comforter. Her eyes were continually drawn to the material...her pajamas.

Despite herself, she traced her fingers across the collar. A sigh came from deep inside her, the place that was so hollow, the place Kurt now filled.

What was wrong with her?

She meant nothing to him. Just because she'd moved backward and felt him against her, it didn't mean he wanted *her*. It meant he was a red-blooded male. Any woman would do, right?

But for a minute or two, in his room, she'd wanted to think it was about her. She stared at the shirt for a long time, until the pattern blurred. Once upon a time, she'd believed Sam cared for her, too.

Kurt had promised not to seduce her when he'd drawn her into his room. Only she knew how much she'd wanted exactly that—to feel like a woman, a beautiful, desired woman.

That was for others, though. Not her.

He'd been right last night: She was still a girl who dreamed of being loved by a prince.

Determined, she stood. She refused to feel sorry for herself. All she had to do was make it through a few days, tell Kurt thanks for the impromptu vacation, then go to Denver on Wednesday.

She wondered why that thought held less appeal than it had just yesterday.

After taking off her clothes, she reached for his shirt. Impossibly the scent of him clung to it, filling her senses. It skimmed her bare breasts, and her nipples tightened into little beads.

She trembled.

Despite what she'd told him earlier about being willing to make love with him, the small taste of passion they'd shared had rocked her to the core. She could never have gone through with it. There was no way possible to survive being with him, skin to naked skin.

She finished changing, the material flowing lower, the hem skirting her thighs and sliding down her hips. Had he worn the same shirt? Had it fit him tighter than it did her? Did it slip between him and his jeans?

Oh, heaven help her. She'd lost her mind.

She couldn't stay here, not another day, not another minute. She couldn't think these things, wonder, be filled with a forbidden longing...

Jessie resolved to leave, the sooner the better.

From experience, she knew the problem would come in getting past him.

Make herself at home, he'd invited. Easier said than done, when his home was closer to a lion's den, and she was the main course.

Six

"**M**orning."

Jessie stood, rooted to the spot, her hand curled around the oak banister.

She hadn't expected to see him. Laying in bed for long minutes, she'd listened carefully for any sound of him. The house had roared with quiet.

Finally, having convinced herself that he'd left for the day, she'd pulled on her jeans, tucked in his shirt and padded barefoot down the stairs.

Only to find him there.

He sat on the floor, back braced against the wall. He wore only a flannel shirt—unbuttoned—and dark blue jeans, jeans that—heavens—weren't even snapped. His feet were bare and Sunshine's head rested on his lap. With repetitive motions, he continually stroked behind the dog's ear and continued down her neck.

He completely captivated Jessie's attention.

Sunshine looked at Jessie and thumped her tail once, before giving a soft whimper and returning to Kurt's soothing ministration.

"Figured she might want some company," Kurt said.

A growth of beard covered his chin and his eyes looked blurry, as if he hadn't slept all night.

"She's in labor?" Jessie asked.

"Yeah."

In that moment, she was lost.

She'd spent the night determined to get away from him, enumerating his faults while trying to forget the way she'd responded to his tender touch.

Counting his faults had been easy; it started with his rejection, continued with the kidnapping and ended with him taking her into his bedroom and standing her in front of a mirror, exposing her completely.

Yet her own part in what had happened haunted her most. Even though she'd protested, saying she didn't want to be in his room, her body had betrayed her time and again.

She'd spent a restless night tossing and turning, trying to get comfortable. It had been impossible. As if it had been kissed by fire, her skin tingled everyplace his hands had touched.

Sometime after midnight, she'd finally given up and crawled out of bed to put her bra back on, unable to stand even the tiniest brush of cotton against her breasts. After that, sleep had still only arrived in broken spurts. Sensual dreams teased her every time she closed her eyes.

This morning, she still wore his shirt. For some reason she hadn't wanted to take it off. Unwilling to examine the real reasons why, she told herself it was because hers had been worn for a whole day, making it dirty. She ignored the nagging voice that reminded her she'd *slept* in his.

"You any good at making coffee?" he asked. His voice
rubbed rawly across his vocal cords, grated and gritty.
"Been waiting for you to get up."

"Just for the coffee?

He shook his head. "Wanted to make sure you were
okay."

"I'm fine." She wondered if he recognized the lie. She'd
never been less fine in her entire life. She'd never had a
man's hands on her breasts, never had her nipples fondled
and teased. She'd never been kissed. Fine definitely didn't
describe how she felt.

"You sure?" he asked.

"Why wouldn't I be?"

He looked at her carefully, then shrugged. "Why
wouldn't you be," he agreed.

"I'm a big girl, capable of making my own decisions.
You were trying to prove a point, and you did. Lesson
learned." Now, if she could only convince herself.

"There was more to it than that, Jess. And you know
it."

She swallowed, knowing she was sinking...losing control.

For a few seconds, he said nothing more. Finally, evi-
dently content to let it go, he asked, "So how 'bout it? Will
you take pity on me and brew a pot of coffee?"

The drive to save herself from him battled the need to
be helpful. Kurt knew her weaknesses, knew she couldn't
refuse to do a favor.

"How strong?"

"You know how they serve it at the Chuckwagon?
That's about right."

Slowly she uncurved her hand from the banister and
moved into the living room. She meant to bypass him, go
straight into the kitchen. She didn't.

Instead, enraptured by the sight of him and the laboring dog, Jessie crouched next to them, scratching Sunshine's ear while he continued to ease his hand down the swollen length of her stomach.

"How long have you been here?" she asked, looking at him.

"Since about three." He stroked Sunshine again. "Easy girl. Won't be long now." Meeting Jessie's gaze, he explained, "I heard her whimper."

Jessie closed her eyes. He was a rancher, a man accustomed to the cycle of life, and he still got up with his pregnant dog because he didn't want her to be alone.

This side of Kurt tantalized her, made her realize intuition had guided her right when she'd asked him to father her child...but that's where her instincts had ended.

Kurt would no more be able to walk away from his child, pretend it wasn't his, than she would.

As he'd pointed out, she'd made a huge mistake.

"The coffee?" he prompted.

Right now, Jessie would give him anything he asked for.

Nodding sharply, she hurried to the kitchen, shutting the door behind her. What was it about him?

What was it about her?

Armed with a mental list of his numerous faults, she was supposed to be plotting her escape, not getting in deeper and deeper.

Telling herself she only had to survive the next couple of hours, that somehow she'd figure out a way to lie to him and get away with it, she pushed her hair back from her face and moved toward the coffeepot.

Jessie waited until the last drop splashed on top of the filled carafe before getting down a mug. She was wasting time. She knew it, yet that was better than being the focus of his intense attention.

This morning felt far too intimate. Neither of them were properly dressed. Combining that with the knowledge of what had happened last night, and the fact they'd slept, separated only by a closed door, left her reeling with vulnerability.

She wasted some more time, cleaning up the mess from their uneaten dinner. Knowing he was waiting and that she'd taken ten minutes longer than necessary, she drew a fortifying breath, then carried a steaming mug into the living room. Once there, she lowered herself to her knees next to him.

"An angel in blue jeans," he murmured. He looked up at her. "Thank you."

This close to him, she was all too aware of his potent masculinity. A downy layer of hair dusted his chest, stretching across the breadth of him and meandering down, disappearing beneath his waistband.

She forced herself to refocus, looking at his face instead. Then she wished she'd studied something less compelling. The never-been-to-sleep look lent him a dangerously sinful air.

Suddenly she felt like sinning.

"Your coffee'll get cold," she said hurriedly.

"So it will."

He didn't stop looking at her, and she swallowed deeply, making excuses to go to the kitchen for her own cup, and more, to hide.

Over the years, her survival instincts had become well honed. She'd needed them to make it through year after year of being passed around, like an unwanted present people weren't sure what to do with. Somehow she'd managed through the turbulent teen years, getting her own apartment when she was barely eighteen.

So where were those same instincts now that she so desperately needed them?

Her hand trembled when she poured hot coffee into a mug. Kurt had been dangerous last night. This morning, he was devastating. He affected her emotionally, making her want love with a hunger that threatened to devour her.

He affected her physically, with a yearning that made her think, for the first time, that she truly was a normal woman with wants.

"Jess—"

His urgent whisper from the living room reached her, jolting her.

"Come here."

Resolutely she gathered courage. Squaring her shoulders, she returned, her false smile becoming real when she saw Sunshine licking the first, newborn puppy.

Putting her coffee on an end table, she dropped to her knees, filled with wonder.

"Your first birth?"

Nodding, she looked at Kurt, seeing softness in his expression. Grim determination had been replaced with something she couldn't name, lightening his green eyes to the color of spring and promise.

His lips were no longer set in a single line, rather they were curved upward. He no longer resembled the man who held her prisoner in his home; instead, he was the person she thought she knew—caring, compassionate.

This was the Kurt she cared about.

For her own sake, she wanted the new Kurt back, the man who frustrated and irritated. She didn't trust herself around his compassion.

"I never get tired of it," he confessed. "Birth, hope."

With great care, she asked, "And what about having kids of your own? Someone to pass the ranch on to?"

"Jessie," he warned, the word a low growl.

"I'm not asking anything more than a simple question."

Dulled maybe, by a long night and quiet morning, he finally said, "I'd need to fall in love first." His brows knitted together. "And that's not likely to happen."

"Belinda did a number on you, didn't she?"

"Betrayal isn't my poison of choice."

She winced. Then, when she might have asked more, the second puppy was born. "Oh, Kurt." The first nuzzled its mother, seeking milk, while Sunshine cared for the newest arrival. "I'm glad I got to see this."

"Yeah," he agreed easily. "I'm glad you did, too."

Thirty minutes and three cups of coffee later, the fifth and final puppy emerged, this one so much tinier than the rest, a different mix of colors, with a black smudge on its head resembling a half-moon.

"It's...precious," Jessie murmured.

"It's the runt."

She frowned at him, finding that his eyes danced with devilment, not matching the seriousness of his tone. "It's cute," she protested.

"Cute?"

She nodded emphatically.

"Maybe in a few days."

"It's cute now," she insisted.

He grinned. "Doesn't surprise me that you'd root for the runt of the litter."

"Something wrong with that?"

"Not at all."

All the pups snuggled up to Sunshine's warmth and the relieved mother gratefully closed her eyes.

"We all need a champion."

Even you? But as much as she wanted to ask the question, she didn't dare.

"When she's old enough, she's yours."

"The runt?" Jessie asked in surprise.

He nodded.

"Mine?"

"As long as you want her."

Her breath expelled. He couldn't have known that having a pet was part of her dreams, a dog to romp around with her kids... With his offer, he'd given her a gift she'd treasure. "Want her? Yes, yes, yes, yes!" Her heart swelling with joy, she impulsively leaned forward. Bracing one hand on his bare chest, she kissed him on the cheek.

Jessie's pulse stopped.

What had she done?

In a moment of recklessness, she'd taken all of her resolutions and thrown them into a westerly wind.

Oh, no.

When her heart began beating again, it was in triple time and she couldn't breathe. "I'm—I'm sorry."

His eyes narrowed, darkened and threatened.

She gulped.

Kurt captured her hand and held it paralyzed. His other hand clamped on her shoulder, biting her skin with strength.

She couldn't think, didn't know what to say, didn't know what to do.

Tears swam into her eyes, blurring her vision. Color clawed its way up her neck and into her cheeks. Foolish, foolish woman, she chided herself.

"I've got chores."

Without another word, he dropped her hand. Releasing her shoulder, he stood. He went upstairs, never looking back at her again.

The bedroom door slammed and she jumped. Sunshine startled and Jessie muttered nonsense in dulcet tones, trying to distract the dog as well as herself.

Sunshine returned to her newborns. Now if Jessie could only be soothed as easily.

She couldn't believe she'd made an idiot out of herself over a man, twice. She knew that she wasn't attractive to a man, any man. How much clearer did Kurt need to make it? Despite his actions last night, his clipped, "I've got chores" spoke louder.

Her shoulders fell forward and the first of the tears slipped from her eyes. She'd been right earlier. She had to get out of here, away from him, before she sank in a sea of her own humiliation.

Kurt pulled a shirt over his head, cursing as he got dressed.

What had nearly happened down there was inexcusable.

Deprived of sleep, he hadn't been on guard. Otherwise he wouldn't have let her get that close. After last night, he already knew she was a forecast of potentially devastating destruction.

He'd gone to bed, not that it had done any good. More than hard, his body was ready. Images of her had slinked across his mind, and he'd pictured her taking off her shirt, replacing it with his, her nipples straining against the fabric.

This morning hadn't been any better.

He'd kept Sunshine company. The whole time, Jessie's ridiculous proposal taunted him. He thought of his words two days earlier, of how he'd impregnate her.

Skin to naked skin.

Hell, yes. That's what he wanted, hard and fast, soft and sensual.

He wanted her.

And last night and again this morning, he'd come close to taking her.

She'd crept down the stairs, pink toenails peeking from

beneath her jeans. Her hair hung in morning disarray around her face. Rather than having the urge to tame it, he'd only wanted to muss it more. She'd buttoned her shirt—his shirt—all the way to the top, but that didn't matter. *He knew what she felt like underneath the cotton.*

She was a banquet for his senses, and every one of his senses prickled with awareness.

Kurt reached for a belt, threading the loops and telling himself the bulge in his jeans didn't matter. He was a grown man. He could handle a little deprivation.

His mind accepted the declaration; his body was another matter. Damn if the scent of her perfume didn't seem to linger in the room.

She'd touched him, her hand on his chest, fingers splayed into his hair. He might have been able to stand that. Fact was, he'd only gotten slightly hard from that.

But then she had to go and lean forward, her hair brushing him, his shoulder, his neck, his chest. The satiny strands had been every bit as erotic as he'd thought they would be.

And her kiss... He shoved his feet into his boots with more force than necessary. Her kiss was so *real*. Heartfelt, emotional, grateful.

It had taken strength he didn't know he possessed to lock his hand around her wrist and stop her before he gave into the primal urges clawing his belly.

He'd seen the rejection in her eyes, knew what she was thinking. Cursing himself to the coast and back, he hadn't been able to spare the time to tell her she was wrong, prove that she was attractive enough to drive any man, and God help him, especially him, wild.

If he'd let her continue, for even two more seconds, he would have taken her hand and moved it lower, placing her palm on him, encouraging her to close her hand around him...

As close to the edge as he was, he'd have lost control.

He'd have shocked every one of her sensibilities. Not only that, but it wouldn't—couldn't—have stopped there.

He wanted her. With the fire burning in his gut, he wanted to possess her.

But she was intended for another man, someone who would love her the way she deserved.

That man was not Kurt Majors.

He wasn't fit for any woman, particularly one who wore her heart in her eyes. He had no desire to get involved again, not anything serious, anyway. And Jessie said serious, in capital letters.

Grabbing his keys from the dresser, he headed into her bedroom. What he was doing was just another inexcusable action, but since he was making a list, he might as well build on it. He knew she'd run; he'd seen it in her eyes. And even though he'd asked, Jessie hadn't promised she'd cancel her appointment once and for all.

That meant he couldn't let her go.

Her shoes under his arm, he headed down the stairs and straight out the front door, ignoring the way her presence seemed to permeate the atmosphere.

He'd hurt her several times already. He knew it...wished he hadn't. But rejection was the lesser of the evils churning inside him. When he was capable of reining in his desires, he'd explain that to her, tell her she got to him, not only that, but she'd get to any normal man.

Yeah, he'd tell her all that, as soon as he was capable, like after he'd exhausted himself on the range. In the saddle. Bareback.

Climbing behind the wheel of his pickup truck, he slammed the door, then gunned the engine, the tires spewing chunks of mud from last night's storm.

He'd never run from a problem before. Not even when

he caught Belinda in the act of making a mockery of the marriage vows he'd taken seriously.

But comparing the two women was as useless as trying to rid his thousand acres of weeds.

Jessie cherished the very things Belinda vilified. Home and hearth mattered to Jessie. Until Belinda, they'd mattered to Kurt, too.

Seeing the sheriff's cruiser on the outskirts of Columbine Crossing, Kurt eased off the accelerator—wasn't in enough time to avoid flashing lights, though.

After pulling over, he drummed his fingers impatiently on the dashboard.

"Kurt—" Spencer McCall said with a brief nod. He thumbed the brim of his battered hat and pulled up the collar of his leather jacket against the still-furious bite of the wind. "Anything wrong?"

More than Spencer would have guessed. "Sorry," Kurt apologized. "Speed got away from me."

Spencer grinned. "Lucky for you, I'm not out for county revenue enhancement."

Kurt tried to grin at his old friend and failed.

"You coming to the poker game this week?"

Now that he was a bachelor, he rarely missed the monthly boys' poker game at Spencer's. But not this week. Not when Jessie was waiting at his house.

He shook his head.

"You sure everything's okay?"

"Early morning." No sleep and an insistent nagging in his groin. A woman snuggled under blankets in a bed next door to his room. Everything was fine. Just fine. "Sunshine had her pups."

"You got up with that mangy mutt?"

"Man's gotta do what a man's gotta do."

Spencer shook his head. "Watch the speed, Kurt."

"Gotcha." Unwilling to push his luck, he did just that.

In town, he stopped in the feed store, picked up a few small dog bowls along with a bag of puppy food for the future, then he impulsively crossed the street to the general store.

Jessie's words about never having had a birthday party reverberated in his mind. After being such a jerk, he could at least give her something good to remember. She deserved it. Hell, she deserved a lot of good things. Unfortunately, for now, she was stuck with him.

He bought a cake, a card and some noisemakers. Then he stopped in front of the gift shop, a stuffed animal in the window grabbing his attention. He recalled Jessie's story, how she'd had nothing but a teddy bear to call her own when she was growing up.

He knew the bear would appeal to her. And he needed to buy her a present. A party wasn't much without presents.

Juggling the bags from his other purchases, he went inside and bought it, sidestepping Angelina's hinted questions as she tried to figure out who the gift was for.

After putting everything in the truck, he headed to the Chuckwagon Diner. Food would cure one of his hungers. He hoped.

Bridget, the Chuckwagon's owner, waited on him. Then as soon as his hands were warming around the brown ceramic cup, Nick Andrews slid into the booth across from Kurt.

"You look like hell."

"Morning to you, too, Nick."

"So what's her name?"

Kurt scowled. "Who?"

"The woman who kept you up all night." He signaled to Bridget, pointing at Kurt's mug. "'Bout time, too."

"Sunshine."

Nick grinned. "Shoulda figured."

Kurt didn't answer. Nick had been Kurt's friend for more years than either could remember. Kurt doubted he'd have survived his divorce with any shred of sanity, if it hadn't been for Nick. Nick had helped Kurt load Belinda's stuff into a moving van, and then Nick had insisted on driving the van to Denver himself, saying Kurt had suffered enough.

Later that night, Nick had returned with a case of beer and had stayed until dawn. As far as friends went, Kurt figured they didn't get much more loyal than Nick Andrews.

The two men discussed a trip they planned to take together to a cattle auction. Then as soon as he'd finished eating, Kurt excused himself.

"You sure her name's Sunshine?" Nick asked, dark brows drawing over blue eyes.

Kurt put his hat on, then dropped a ten on the table.

Before heading back home, he stopped in at the post office.

Inserting his key into the ancient brass lock of the small box—good thing he knew its location, since the numbers had worn off a decade ago—he opened the small door, the hinges growling in protest.

The slot was empty except for a note, asking him to call at the window to pick up a package.

He crossed the ancient lobby. The post office looked pretty much the way it had when it was built, sometime in the late fifties.

Bernadette Simpson, the postmistress, was said to have arrived the same day as the first piece of mail. He didn't know whether to believe the legend or not, but the fact was, no one in town, not even the senior residents, remembered a time Bernadette hadn't delivered the mail, along with a healthy dose of gossip.

Speculation had it that Bernadette was none other than the *Courier*'s mysterious columnist, Miss Starr. After all, who better than the town's postmistress to know everyone's business, from birthday cards to past due notices on the electric bill?

Still, Bernadette's name occasionally showed up in the column, too, leaving the townsfolk to wonder if their guesses really were right.

"Young man! There you are," Bernadette said, interrupting her conversation with Lillian Baldwin, co-owner of Rocky Mountain Floral and Landscaping. "Didn't know when we'd see the likes of you again."

"Thought of you and just had to make a special trip to town."

"Ah," she said. "A man after my own heart."

He grinned at her and was rewarded with a coy smile in return. Some people, he decided, were easy to please. Left him wondering why the older woman was still single after all these years. Surely there was a gentleman somewhere interested in the still vivacious woman.

"I'll see you later," Lillian said to Bernadette.

"Thanks for the book and the flowers," Bernadette said.

"I remembered that pink carnations are your favorite."

Bernadette traced her finger across the petals, seemingly lost in thought. "Jonathan used to bring them to me."

"Jonathan?" Kurt asked.

Bernadette shook her head and blinked. "It was a long time ago, so never you mind."

He exchanged a glance with Lillian, and Bernadette pretended not to notice.

"Maybe you'd like to stop by Lillian's shop, sometime," Bernadette said to Kurt, arching her brow.

"For?"

"Flowers. Every woman loves them. Don't they, Lillian?"

Lillian smothered a laugh, but added, "Bernadette's right. You can never go wrong with flowers, Kurt. It's amazing how much they soften a woman's heart. I'll even give you a first-timer's discount." With a few more polite words, Lillian wiped her hand down the side of her flowing skirt, then excused herself.

The ancient door creaked behind Lillian, the wind catching the wood and whipping it against the frame. And that left him as the focus of Bernadette Simpson's attention.

He slid the yellow slip of paper onto the counter and she took a few moments to grab the pile of mail, secured by a rubber band. There was no package.

She kept her hand on the bundle and whispered, "You're right, there is no package. This—" she nodded at the official notification form "—was a ruse."

If she didn't seem so serious, he would have chuckled. "A ruse?" he asked, lowering the pitch of his voice to match hers.

"I needed to speak privately with you." With a surreptitious glance around the lobby, she leaned closer to him. "I wanted to have the chance to ask you about Jessica Stephens firsthand."

Tension gripped the back of his neck. "What about her?"

"Mrs. Johnson—you know, Jessica's neighbor..."

Yes, he did know. He sighed. He remembered all too clearly her expression of intense curiosity two mornings ago.

"Well, Mrs. Johnson was in here yesterday. It seems Jessica hasn't been home, and well, I know this is incredible, but..." She trailed off to clear her throat and look at the empty lobby one more time. "Well, anyway, she's getting worried, and you know, she isn't nearly as circumspect in gossiping as I am."

He thrummed impatient fingers on smooth wood, worn down, he imagined, from others doing exactly what he was doing right now.

"Mercy, Kurt..." She dropped her voice even lower, making it barely audible. "That busybody, she'd have us all believing you kidnapped that poor girl."

He raked his hand into his hair. "Kidnapped?"

"Outrageous, I know," she sympathized, placing her aged hand on top of his. "You wouldn't know anything about it, now would you?"

He said nothing.

"Guess Mrs. Johnson's going to talk to the sheriff soon if Jessica doesn't come home."

He nearly groaned aloud.

She squeezed his hand with more strength than he would have believed possible. Then she cocked her head to one side. When she spoke again, it was still quiet, but strength wound through her whisper. "Take care of her, young man, and I mean it. I'll try and keep Mrs. Johnson out of your way, but if anything happens to that little one, I'll call Spencer McCall myself."

A pulse throbbed in Kurt's temple.

"Am I perfectly clear, Mr. Majors?"

"Yes, ma'am." Taking care of Jessie would be as easy as stringing barbed wire, now that half the town knew she'd been kidnapped and the other half had probably heard the rumors.

He exhaled and Bernadette moved the pile of mail toward him. "Mercy me, it's going to be another cold one tonight. Hear tell there's another storm system pushing in from the north. Someone needs to tell the weather it's supposed to be spring.'' She shivered for effect.

His head spun.

He'd been warned and threatened, now she was discussing the weather.

Women.

When he thought he'd figured them out, they changed the rules. One thing was certain; he had to convince Jessie to drop the insane plan of having a baby out of wedlock.

At this point, he knew he had to use whatever tactics he could, fair or foul. He was running out of time. It wouldn't be much longer before the town's well-meaning residents mounted a rescue mission.

With energy bordering on desperation, he headed home. To Jessie.

Bernadette watched the young man leave, a small smile toying at the corner of her lips.

The boy was smitten.

Oh, yes indeed, he most certainly was.

And now, with the way he hadn't denied kidnapping young Jessica, Bernadette would be willing to place bets that Kurt Majors was going to be a daddy.

Mercy! What a stroke of brilliance it had been to ask him to call at the window. Kurt was notoriously closed-mouthed. He hadn't even breathed a single word about his divorce.

Angelina from the gift shop chose that moment to walk into the post office, bubbling with excitement.

"Guess what?" Angelina whispered conspiratorially.

Wisely Bernadette made sure they were alone before leaning over the counter. "A stuffed bear?" she asked a few seconds later, thoughtfully tapping her finger against her chin. "Hmm." She thanked her source—even though Angelina would never realize she'd been a source.

When Angelina hurried off to share the news, Miss Starr pulled out her quill and a piece of parchment paper, hurriedly penning an article. Ten minutes later, she smiled gleefully. She'd scored a coup and nothing felt better.

Hurrying to the newspaper offices, she turned in her masterpiece.

Back outside, the frigid wind stole air from her lungs, but she didn't mind. Spring was on its way, even if the weather forecasters disagreed.

She looked down the street.

The church graced the end of Front Street, its whitewashed walls patiently waiting for the bells to toll in joy. And if Miss Starr was granted her wish, those bells would surely ring soon!

With a final wistful look at the church, she turned toward the post office, but was halted when Trudy Jackson called out from across the street.

Wondering if Trudy had relented yet and agreed to date the scandalously younger Henry Belaforte, of Henry's Snips and Clips, Bernadette waved. Mercy, at Trudy's age, a little thing like a few years shouldn't matter. Maybe, Bernadette thought, she could do something to help in that quarter.

Then it was on to Lillian. Poor girl hadn't dated since she came home two years ago. It was high time she got on with life. With a sigh, Bernadette went inside once more. Every action needed a plan, and that's exactly what she intended to do.

Jessie paced the kitchen, anger building with every step.

The pickup's back wheels had spun furiously when Kurt had left, spitting mud into a huge cloud of brown.

She had closed her eyes in frustration, then firmly decided she'd had enough. Nothing was going to stop her from leaving today and getting on with her life, even if she had to walk all the way back to town.

She'd showered and dressed, then hunted for her shoes. But, even after fifteen minutes of determined searching, she hadn't found them.

That meant one thing. Kurt—confound him—had taken them.

Her mind supplied a dozen different, imaginative names for him.

He'd stranded her, keeping her prisoner. And anger built with every passing minute.

Fury didn't even begin to describe how she felt.

With a huge sigh, she pushed her bangs back from her forehead. A storm was brewing outside the house. Inside it as well.

Kurt had more than a few things to answer for.

A vehicle engine droned in the distance, then the sound of thunder drowned out his approach.

She'd heard enough, though, to know he was returning. It was about time. She was ready—more than ready.

Jessie crossed to the front door, her feet warmed only by her socks. She stood in the open doorway, the wind whipping at her hair and tossing it around her face.

Anger simmered around her, fed by frustration and refined by rejection. What right did he have to keep her here, against her will, making decisions for her life, then turning around and walking out?

He had no power in her life, and she intended to tell him so, in no uncertain terms.

Folding her arms across her chest and trying to still the thumping of her heart, she waited for him, anxious to unleash the brewing storm.

Seven

"**Y**ou've got nerve, Kurt Majors."

Her words hung frostily on the churning early-afternoon air. "Me?" he asked innocently, shocked and more than a little intrigued by the spitfire standing in his doorway, blue eyes flashing fire and mouth set in a firm line...a line he knew he could curve with a single stroke of his mouth across hers.

"And I have more than a few things to say to you."

He held the bag of doggy bowls in one hand, but he'd left the birthday surprise in the pickup. Maybe it was a good thing.

At a loss of how to deal with this new, unexpected Jessie, he asked, "Can I come in?"

"No."

"No?"

"Hell, no."

His jaw slackened. Hell, no? From Jessie?

She pushed a finger against his chest. "Was that clear enough, or should I spell it out for you?"

The heat of Jessie's hostility seared him.

He'd been prepared for several reactions when he returned, hurt, frustration, upset, but this... He flinched with the realization that he was the recipient. "Jessie, look—"

"No, Kurt, you look. I've been kidnapped, held against my will and I've had enough." She dug her finger deeper into him. "I've had enough of your caveman tactics. I'm fed up with you cutting me off and running away."

She stood there, in the middle of the doorway, *his doorway*, not budging, leaving him in the freezing cold. Her hair flickered around her face and her arms were folded just beneath her breasts, emphasizing the way they pressed against the soft cotton of his shirt.

Kurt knew it was a good thing his legs were spread wide, otherwise he had no idea how he'd be able to stand up.

The combination of her heat, with the combustible heat building between them, made him hot. In his entire life, he'd never known a woman who appealed to him this way. "Are you done?" he asked.

"No."

The bag weighed on his hand and the wind whipped through his shirt.

"You have no right to treat me the way you have, humiliate me—"

"Humiliate?" he interrupted, his own temper beginning to simmer.

"Humiliate," she restated, refusing to back down.

"Explain that one to me."

Color crept into her face, but she didn't look away. "You drag me into your bedroom, start undressing me, then you send me off to my own bed. You steal my shoes, keep me prisoner and when I give you an innocent thank-you kiss you freak out and can't get away from here fast enough.''

She drew a breath. To fan the flame? he wondered.

''Sam may have done a number on me, but at least he had the decency to say I didn't turn him on instead of turning tail.''

His anger flashed in that instant. ''Decency?'' The word was bitten with the hard edge of hostility. His nostrils flared. ''Decency?'' he demanded again.

''Yes, decency.''

''Let me tell you about decency, little lady.''

Skin to naked skin. His own words formed a thought that teased him, taunted him. Yeah, he wanted, wanted her.

Then he made a mistake.

He put down the bag. Knocking away her hand, he reached for her, closing his palms around her shoulders.

The atmosphere blazed, and it had nothing to do with the low-lying clouds. Something low and deep in him surged to life.

''Take your hands off me,'' she said, her words dripping with icicles.

''Sure. The second we're done with this little talk that you wanted.'' He pushed her away, then without even glancing back, he caught the door with his heel and gave it a shove, sending it shuddering into its casing. ''Sam had the decency to leave you alone, did he?'' Kurt all but sneered. ''Well, let me tell you about real decency.''

From the kitchen, he heard Sunshine's barked protests.

''Real decency is stopping when you're so damn hard and all you want to do is bury yourself inside a willing woman.''

''Oh, really?''

Her challenge ignited anger he never knew existed inside him. He hadn't been this furious when he'd found Belinda and Daniel in his bed. "Real decency is sending a woman to her own bed before you take her to yours."

"I appreciate the lesson—"

"Real decency is capturing a woman's wrist and holding it instead of moving it to the front of your jeans."

That got her attention.

"You're not a fool, Jessie. You backed into me last night, in front of the mirror." This had been simmering inside since last night, eating him up and demanding a release. "You felt my hardness. Didn't you?"

She swallowed.

"Yeah, I wanted to show you that you weren't an Ice Princess. But I didn't bargain on what it would do to me. The feel of your skin, soft and smooth, against these hardened calluses..." His fingers dug deeper into her skin, making her wince.

"Then you backed up and that was all it took to make me forget how to think. But that wasn't enough." He intentionally let his gaze flick to the swell of her breasts. "I unfastened a few of your buttons, then undid the clasp of your bra.

"There was a reason I stopped, Jessie, a reason I didn't finish undressing you and look at you. And that's because looking wouldn't have been enough. I wouldn't have been satisfied until I touched you more intimately, until I tasted you." Anger blinded him to everything but reaction. "Shocked?"

She didn't respond.

"I would have taken your nipple in my mouth and curled my tongue around the tip."

In his hands, her shoulders dipped.

"Now you tell me," he insisted with lethal quiet. "Should I have sent you to your own room?"

"This wasn't part of our bargain."

"Want to tell me all about it?" He gave her a soft shake. "I know it wasn't part of the bargain. I'm trying to get you to see that you're a desirable woman and that any man would be lucky to have you.

"So I spend a sleepless night convincing myself I've done that. Then you leaned against me, put your hand on my chest and kissed me." He demanded the attention of her gaze. "My erection was instantaneous."

"Kurt—"

"Jessie," he countered. "I wanted to take your pants off and bury myself in you."

She sucked in a hollow breath.

Determinedly he fought to hold himself steady, struggling for patience, something it seemed he didn't have a lot of luck with when it came to her.

In every area of his life, he'd used timing to his best advantage—when it came to buying the ranch, adding to its holdings, purchasing cattle at the lowest possible prices, selling them at the highest. There was something about Jessie, though, that turned his world upside down, made rational thought something only a stronger man was capable of.

Then, she blinked several times and something shifted. Her scent washed over him. She'd showered, and her hair was fresh, her body like summer. Her hair hung softly, femininely, invitingly. "I left so I didn't do any of those things. That was decency," he said. "But this isn't..."

Until that very moment, he hadn't planned on taking her in his arms again, definitely had no thought of kissing her senseless with the same passion she'd triggered in him, had no intention of coaxing a response from her that was so deep it would rock both of them.

He did, regardless. Specifically he did them in that exact

order. "Come here," he said, his words falling somewhere between a question and a command.

Seeing hesitation in the way her tongue took a quick pass across her lip, he moved his hands, placing one between her shoulder blades and the other in the small of her back. "Open your mouth for me, Jessie..."

Unlike the gentleman he thought himself to be, he took advantage of her surprise, sneaking in and touching his tongue against hers.

He inhaled. This time her scent was that of stormy surrender. The untamed part of him responded.

Galvanized, he drove deeper, determinedly. He captured her tiny moan between them.

Exerting more pressure with his hands, he drew her ever closer, her breasts against his chest. Through the layers of fabric separating them, her nipples beaded tightly, the way they had when his thumbs had brushed them.

He'd had his first kiss somewhere around the age of fourteen, and he'd kissed numerous women in the ensuing years. Not one of them had made him this needy.

Urgency clawed at him, building from inside and surging upward, filling him, making him hard.

Her head tipped back to grant him deeper access. Greedily he took it.

Their tongues circled, met, danced, retreated, imitating the intimacy of lovemaking.

Unfortunately his body wanted the real thing.

This, as incredible as it was, should only be a prelude. Yet, with his obligation to her, knowing she was meant for another man, it had to be the final act.

He wished that the mere thought doused the wanting...

Drawing away before the friction of their movements caused something he was loathe to explain, he cradled her head and settled for placing his lips against the pulse shuddering in her throat.

She made a sexy little sound, and it drove him onward once again, despite himself. He moved lower, bringing around his other hand to start slipping buttons out of their protective holes. One of her hands burrowed into his hair. With the other, she grabbed hold of his shoulder, her fingers clutching the fabric of his shirt.

Her response dictated his.

Kissing the skin his hand bared, he watched, thrilled, the way her chest rose and fell, with no regularity. Her breaths were ragged, with long broken inhalations and shaky exhalations. She was all woman, all right…enough for any man who was man enough to enjoy unrestrained passion.

He was that man.

He followed the outline of her bra, feeling her heat, seeing the peaks of her breasts strain against sensible cotton. Something similar was happening within the confines of his denim, too, something he was in danger of losing control over.

Lowering his head, he worked his tongue beneath the fabric, exploring the softness of her flesh. She gasped, holding his head closer. Her back arched and he felt the tightness of her nipple.

Before he was totally lost, he forced himself to stop and take a step back. Blood pounded in him, like a hammer in his skull. "You're a desirable woman, Jessica Stephens. And if I had any less *decency*, I'd show you, right here, right now, just how desirable."

Jessie stood in front of him, numb with shock. He'd turned tables on her completely, taking her anger, building on it until his passion threatened to consume them both.

Her body tingled where his mouth had been, her breasts

filled the cups of her bra and she felt constrained by the fabric.

His words and actions combined to make her want, desperately, to believe him, that she was desirable, that some man might someday want her, and that dreams might truly exist.

The knowledge that she possessed the power to make Kurt want her made her delirious, as if she stood at the top of the world without oxygen.

Heaven help her, having had a hint of the possibilities, she wanted more, so much more. He had uncovered depths of her that she never suspected existed. She'd spent her life burying her true self under layers of who others expected her to be. But no more.

She had to admit that a secret part of her was pleased that she hadn't left Kurt while he was gone, despite her intention of doing just that.

Now, more than ever, she wanted to be held and cradled, touched and stroked. She wanted to learn, about herself, about her body.

And she wanted Kurt to be the man she first made love with.

"Kurt..." The asking was impossible. "Did you mean..."

He looked at her, and she noticed his eyes were the same, darkened green they had been when he'd captured her gaze, right before he kissed her. "Yeah, Jess?"

"I..." Exhaling, she turned away and went to the window where wind battered the panes and rain splattered down in huge pelts. "You said you weren't intent on seducing me."

"Are you trying to get a promise out of me? Because lady, right now I don't think I can give it."

Slowly she faced him. "I'm asking the opposite."

"You what?"

"I want you to teach me, show me, help me."

"Seduce you?"

"I know it's asking a lot—"

"I'm warning you, don't say it." His voice thundered with warning, colliding with the weather. His hands formed tight fists and that telltale thud beat in his temple. "You don't know what you're asking."

"I do." She drew a breath that didn't even begin to fill her lungs. "I want you to make love to me. Teach me how to make love to you."

"This is insane."

She nodded. "Maybe."

"You want to be naked in front of me?"

Her heart added a few extra beats…each second. With huge effort she nodded.

"You want me to hold your breasts, caress them, taste them, make you respond to me?"

Heaven help her.

"And you want me inside you?"

She leaned her shoulders against the window, seeking support. The cold didn't comfort; it just made her ache to be wrapped in his warm arms again.

"That is what you're asking for, isn't it? You, me, us. Skin to naked skin." His voice grated, as if drawn from a well of patience that was quickly drying out.

"Yes," she whispered. "But, please, don't misunderstand, I'm not trying to…trick you or anything. Wanting a baby would have nothing to do with this."

He muttered a quiet curse, adding something about small mercies.

Finding courage, from where, she wasn't sure, Jessie crossed the room toward him, her stocking feet making no sound. In fact, even if she'd been wearing boots, Jessie doubted she'd hear anything above the roar in her head.

She had never acted this way before. Yet she'd come too far, exposed far too much of herself to back down now.

Her fingers spread wide, she placed them on his chest, feeling the heat of him, inhaling the power of him. He towered above her, dwarfing her. She had to tip back her head to look at him properly. When she did, it was to find his gaze unblinkingly focused on her.

His lips were drawn in a straight, formidable line. Was she daring or simply foolish? She didn't know for sure. She only knew that she needed this. She needed him.

She'd always dreamed of saving herself for the man she intended to marry. Unfortunately that man hadn't wanted her. This was her chance to find out if Kurt was right, if she should still take a chance on finding a man.

Jessie moved her hand slowly up, trying to pretend it wasn't shaking. Snagging his top button with her fingernail, she muttered, "Darn it."

"Jessie." His hand closed around hers. "Are you trying to seduce me?"

"I guess it's not working." Tears stung her eyelids.

He traced a finger across her eyebrow. "It's working."

"Then...?"

"Lady, you may be the death of me."

She blinked.

"But if you want to undress me, do it upstairs."

The invitation nearly proved to be her undoing.

In less than half a second, he'd picked her up and was holding her against his chest. "I like it better this way," he said.

She snuggled against him, seeing the pulse in his throat. It matched the speed and irregular rhythm of hers, proving that what he'd said earlier was true—she excited him.

The knowledge was heady, making her feel, for the very first time, like a woman.

She'd had no idea she could feel so alive, vibrant, as if the world's endless possibilities were hers for the choosing.

He carried her up the stairs, his breathing never laboring even though the steps were narrow and steep. At the top, he paused, looking at her.

"My room or yours?" he asked.

Suddenly it became all too real. Her mouth dried.

"Changed your mind?"

"No. Have you?" she managed to say around a tongue that suddenly felt two times too big for her mouth.

"I should. If I was half the gentleman my folks believe me to be, I'd take you back downstairs."

"But?"

"I want to make love to you, Jessie."

Knowing that at least she could escape to the sanctuary of her own room if she needed to, she softly said, "Your room."

He grinned.

The mirror dominated the room. It was an instant, flooding reminder of the night before, of the things she'd learned, the things she still wanted to know.

He carried her to the bed, setting her on the side of the mattress. And Jessie had no idea what to do next. Had this been a mistake?

"Relax," he said.

Nervously she laughed.

"We'll take it slow and easy."

Jessie preferred they just get it over with so she wouldn't have to live through this uncertainty again.

Kurt was having none of that, though.

"Kiss me," he said.

"Kiss...you?"

"I've kissed you, every time, except for this morning. I believe it's your turn."

"I don't know how."

"Just be yourself." He stood several feet away from her, his arms folded across his chest.

He looked handsome, appealing and remote. No, remote wasn't the right word, she mentally amended. *Intent* was better. It was as if he was giving her a chance to change her mind, to set the pace.

She wanted this, she reminded herself.

Standing, she slowly took the two tiny steps needed to bring her to him. Her knees knocked, but his smile gave her the courage she needed. "Will you..." She swallowed and tried again. "Will you unfold your arms?"

"Where do you want them?"

"Around me."

"Around you, how?"

"Like you did earlier."

"Ah, one hand between your shoulder blades and the other in the small of your back so I can hold you against me?"

"Yes."

He did what she asked, the contact between them making her pulse soar.

"Now what?" He feathered the question into her ear, the warmth of his breath stirring her hair along with her senses.

"Hold me tighter."

"My pleasure."

She was no longer sure that's what she wanted. He filled her vision completely, the cotton of his dark blue long-sleeved shirt beckoning her to rest her hands on his chest. Following her instincts, she placed one palm near his buttons.

"What next?" he asked huskily.

"Do I have to do all the work myself?"

"You lead, I'll follow."

But it wasn't a dance, or was it? She rose on her tiptoes and his hands moved with her, guiding her. She fed the fingers of her free hand into his short dark hair, feeling the rich texture. In response, Kurt lowered his head.

Their gazes met. Green eyes were spiked with flecks of gold. She'd seen that once before, last night, when he'd told her what he saw when he looked at her. His nostrils were pinched, as if breathing was difficult.

Lightly, oh, so incredibly lightly, she allowed her lips to touch his. Emboldened, she did it again.

He groaned. Deep inside Jessie experienced a gradual change as warmth unfurled, spreading through her.

Daringly she ran her tongue across his lips.

Then she touched her tongue to his.

The tempo changed.

Kurt took over.

Instead of leading, she followed, surrendering to his demands. Their tongues met, retreated. He'd kissed her like this before, but now she understood. It was so much more than a kiss or an ending. It was a prelude, a beginning.

With a hungry growl, he claimed even more of her mouth. Instead of a slow unfurling, heat rushed through her, consuming her, igniting a fire that flared to her nerve endings.

Driven by something greater than she was able to define, Jessie fought to lower her hand on his chest, reaching for his top button.

After she'd fumbled for several seconds, the blasted button popped free. She slipped her hand inside the opening, exploring his strength.

It wasn't enough. *She wanted more.*

Even as he deepened the kiss and spread his legs wider, she searched for the next button.

Rain pelted the window and wind rattled the wooden casings, as if to echo the moment's urgency.

She tried to wiggle away in order to trail her hand inside his shirt, but he held her steady, his hand moving lower, resting on her behind and drawing her closer into the frame of his spread legs.

She gasped.

He'd told her how he responded to her, and now she felt him, straining and pressing against her stomach. Unconsciously she moved.

Kurt froze. He ended the kiss and stared at her ferociously. "Woman," he warned.

"Ah, um, did I do something wrong?"

"Nothing except trying to end this before it even got started."

"Oh—"

"Jessie, you drive me to distraction," he said, capturing her earlobe and gently nipping.

She cried out. He captured her forward motion, holding her steady.

"Stand still," he said.

"But..."

"Trust me."

His breath was labored against her ear and his chest rose and fell in rapid bursts. He squeezed his eyes closed and Jessie fought to do what he said, even though it took all her self-control. She didn't know exactly what she wanted, but the way they'd moved...it felt good.

He drew a stuttering breath, then expelled it again. "That was a fantasy of mine," he confessed.

She raised questioning brows.

"Feeling your hair across my chest."

He'd had a fantasy? *About her?* Jessie gave thanks for him holding her. If he hadn't been, she might have collapsed against him.

He wound his fingers in her hair, bringing the strands to his lips. "Last chance to back out, Jessie."

The wind momentarily ceased its howling, as if it, too, waited with its breath held.

"Otherwise I'm going to carry you to the bed and make sweet love to you. And I can't promise I'll ever let you go."

Eight

Kurt told himself he was man enough to back off if she said no. Truth to tell, he didn't know if he possessed the ability to keep his hands to himself, not touch her, not hold her, not discover her.

"Yes," she said, the single word making his body react.

He picked her up again, deciding he liked it. Different feel, different view than slinging her over his shoulder. He liked cradling her; it seemed protective. And the way her head burrowed against his shoulder... Well, as he'd told her before, she made a man glad to be a man.

They crossed the room, the sound of her breathing commingling with his.

He sat her on the edge of the bed. This time, he didn't intend to let her up. Wolfishly he grinned. Could be a long night. He *hoped* it would be a long night.

"Buttons first." He tugged the shirt from her jeans and

slowly revealed the creaminess of her skin, seeing her bra, then the outline of her rib cage.

She looked up, her eyes wide and expressive, offering trust, but flares of darker blue wondering what she'd gotten herself into. Her mouth had parted slightly, making him recall the way her mouth tasted, not that he'd ever come close to forgetting.

He shucked the shirt from her shoulders, letting the fabric fall. "Stand up, Jessie." Didn't matter all of a sudden that he'd been determined to keep her in bed. He wanted to see her, every inch of her as he removed her clothes.

He offered his hand, hoping she wouldn't notice that it trembled. Men, grown men, didn't tremble. He never had, until now.

She gave her hand, and his closed around her smaller one. It was damp, he noticed, slick. For every bit that she affected him, he affected her.

The knowledge fed his masculine ego.

Instead of reaching for her bra, he chose to savor her unveiling. He flicked open the top metal button of her jeans, and she sucked in a breath when his fingers came in contact with her belly.

Soft. Womanly. And he was wanting...

He dragged the zipper down, each yielding pull a promise. Patience ebbed; he knew he neared its end.

Having to bend to accomplish his task, he pulled down her jeans, trailing kisses over her. "Step out of them," he urged.

Denim landed on top of flannel.

"Socks," he said, giving thanks he'd taken her shoes.

Standing, he took a step away, allowing his gaze to trail down her body. Clad only in bra and panties, both of the not-expecting-to-be-with-a-man variety—something, surprisingly, he liked—she pulled back her shoulders. He read the rigidity there, testimony to her apprehension. "Beautiful," he murmured, meaning it. And to him, she was. Sensational.

"I'm not—"

He shook his head. "You're perfect."

Wind made the window shimmer and light cast its reflection across the room, into the corners and across her. "Will you take off your bra for me?"

He saw the gulp she swallowed. "I held you last night, felt you. Now I want to see you, watch you."

"I—er..."

"For me, Jessie?"

She nodded and the movement of her head caused long strands of hair to shelter her shoulders.

If guts won a prize, she'd deserve a trophy.

How different she was from his ex-wife. Belinda, always selfish, would have rolled her eyes at his request. Then, when he held back, she would have sensed it and resented it. She would have wanted him to get it over with, the quicker the better, as if being in bed with him was the supreme sacrifice.

To her, it probably had been. The sooner she kicked him out from beneath the covers, the sooner she could move Daniel in.

Kurt's jaw tightened.

"Kurt?"

"I'll try to be patient."

She laughed nervously. "The expression on your face doesn't agree."

"Stay there," he said, crossing to the bed. He sat there uncomfortably, having to adjust his fly once, followed by a second time. "Okay, I'm the picture of patience." On the outside, maybe.

Her hands shook as she reached for the clasp. Her brows

drew together, probably feeling as though her fingers were all thumbs. Finally he heard the nearly imperceptible sound of metal surrendering.

She shrugged, discarding the bra, instantly folding her arms across herself.

Patience. It chose today, of all days, to desert him.

He formed two fists. Didn't help. Only increased the tension in his body. As if he needed that.

Long moments later, she slowly lowered her arms. Less than two feet away from him, a distance he could devour in less than a second, she stood there, giving him one of the greatest gifts he'd ever been given—a sweet woman's trust.

Her breasts were perfect, not large, but as he'd discovered last night, they were just the right size for him to cradle in his palms. Her nipples were rigid peaks, and more than ever he wanted a taste.

He didn't know who he was torturing, him or her.

Kurt squeezed his eyes closed. Didn't really matter. Control was a lasso he couldn't throw.

When he opened his eyes, it was to find she'd closed hers. Her brows were furrowed together, a study in apprehension.

"Jessie…?"

She looked at him. "I haven't changed my mind." She sighed. "I'm just…" She blinked several times. "Nervous."

"There's no need."

"I'm afraid you won't want me."

"Lady, I guarantee you, that's not going to happen."

Seeming to find resolve, if not courage, she slid her hands beneath the elastic of her panties and removed them.

A breath hissed out from his closed teeth. Good thing he was still dressed. That was the only thing keeping him from entering her in a single stroke. "Now come here," he commanded quietly.

"You're not disappointed?"

The raggedness in her voice tore through him. She'd offered herself to another man and he hadn't cherished her. Anger at Bucket collided with Kurt's own desire to show her how wonderful she truly was. "No, Jessie. I'm not disappointed."

She wavered forward before locking her knees to catch herself.

He saw just how important that moment was to her. How much determination had it taken, he wondered, for her to offer herself so completely to him? "I'll show you." He welcomed her into the hollow where he spread his legs. Wrapping one arm around her, he kissed her, below her rib cage.

She wiggled backward, her gasp hanging in the air above him. In just a few seconds, he'd moved her to the bed and started pulling off his boots. He cursed their fit. Until now, he'd never experienced this kind of trouble before.

With unabashed curiosity, she watched him. Belinda never had. If there was even a single similarity between the two women, he couldn't find it.

He thumbed back his belt buckle, but didn't waste time pulling the leather from the denim loops. He barely took the time to yank the zipper all the way down—then when metal teeth took bites, he wished he'd tried to find a bit more of that damnable patience.

His clothes tossed on top of hers in a careless heap, Kurt joined her on the bed, propping on an elbow to peruse her.

Drawing a deep, distracting breath, he reached for one of her breasts, closing his hand around it and feeling its tip against one of his calluses. She moaned. The sound shot right through him and blood pulsated demandingly in his groin.

The distracting breath hadn't helped.

He drew his thumb across her nipple, feeling the change as it pebbled for him.

"Kurt..." She arched her hips toward him.

"Soon," he promised. "I want to be sure you're ready."

"I am."

He chuckled. Then he turned his attention to her other breast. Holding it, he allowed its weight to rest fully in the cup of his hand.

When he touched his tongue to her, she screamed.

"What...?" she asked groggily.

"You wanted to learn," he said quietly, even the whisper seeming to echo in the simmering atmosphere. His breath washed across the dampness of her skin. "I want to learn about you...what you like, how you respond."

"Can't you, can't you experiment later?"

She was a wonder, this Jessie. He'd never suspected her numerous depths, the passion that hid behind light blue eyes. He intended to enjoy every step of the discovery, though. "What is it you want?" he asked.

"For you to make love to me."

"I am."

Her eyes widened, but she said nothing.

"I want to make every part of you satisfied, Jessie."

"They are."

He'd wanted her since he'd taken hold of her when she'd come to him with her ridiculous proposal. That demand hadn't diminished.

"Kurt. Please...now..."

Wanting to prolong the build up, but no longer able to, he reached for a box in the nightstand drawer, absently wondering if they ever expired. It had been a long time...

After slipping on the protection, he returned to her, noticing she hadn't stopped looking at him, following every one of his motions.

He stroked the inside of her thigh and her legs parted. With smooth motions, he moved higher until he felt her feminine warmth.

"Kurt!"

His pulse thundered in his ears, drowning out thought. Gently separating her folds, he checked to make sure she was ready, that he wouldn't hurt her.

Her legs started to close as she dug her heels into the mattress. "Relax," he said soothingly.

Seconds later, with an expelled breath, she did.

He moved his fingers across her most sensitive spot and she arched toward him. He built a rhythm between them, slow, then faster. When a whimper tore from her, he moved between her legs, seeking entrance.

Jessie moaned when his tip entered her.

"You okay?" His weight on his elbows, he didn't know if he'd ever done anything more difficult than stopping.

"Just... I don't know what to do."

"You don't have to." His elbows wobbled. "If you want me to stop, tell me."

"I'm okay." Drawing her lower lip into her mouth, she nodded.

"Almost there," he said, feeling her, the way she surrounded him, in invitation.

A final push passed the final resistance, and he sank his entire length into her. He froze. "Jessie?" His voice dragged, raw, past his vocal cords. "You were a virgin?"

He shouldn't have been surprised, all the signs were there. But he'd assumed she and Sam had gone the entire way, without Sam being able to climax. "Jessie, damn it, answer me."

"Are you angry?"

A million different thoughts impacted, but anger wasn't one of them. "No. Why didn't you say something?"

"I thought you'd know."

"You should have saved this for the man you're going to marry."

Tension, thick as Colorado's cloudy atmosphere, dropped over them.

"Please, Kurt. It's too late now."

Frustration devoured all his other emotions. What the hell had he done?

She was innocent, he'd known that, but pure as well?

He exhaled. Maybe he was angry, but it was turned against himself, not her.

Her arms reached around him. "Don't..."

He saw the tears that swam across her eyes, threatening her eyelashes.

"Don't you reject me, too."

Kurt doubted he'd ever faced a more difficult decision. He shouldn't do this. In this moment, though, he could deny her nothing.

Her hands tangled in his hair. "I've never begged for anything in my life."

"Don't," he warned. "I don't want you to."

She waited, shifting as if to accommodate his intrusion.

"I knew what I was asking for, Kurt."

But he hadn't known what she was offering, hadn't known that in making love to her he'd be accepting her most precious gift.

Lowering his head toward her, he feathered a kiss against her cheek. "Jessie..."

And then, his raw and pulsating need swamped him.

Physical urge dominated rational thought. Kurt slowly began to move inside her, watching her.

At his first stroke, her eyes widened. With the second, they fluttered closed, only to open again with his third, the deepest.

Inside him, heat built, low in his belly. He felt the force gathering. He only prayed he lasted long enough to fulfill her before seeking his own release. "Move with me," he encouraged.

Her legs widened as she rode along with him, their motions becoming one.

He felt the changes in her, heard her breath shorten. Kurt focused completely on her, trying to ignore the insistent demand from his own body.

Her hands fell away from him, landing on the sheet beneath her. She bunched the bedsheet in her fists, raising her knees again, seeking purchase with her heels.

Kurt gritted his teeth.

"I..."

He drove into her again, meeting her hips and surging. She cried out and he cursed, allowing his heat to spill.

She called his name, her hair feathering across his pillow.

He'd been right earlier, he knew. She was magnificent, from her honesty to her response.

Right then, uncharitably, he was glad Bucket had had performance anxieties. The idiot had wanted a test drive and didn't even know how to start the engine.

With masculine pride, Kurt was glad he'd been the first to hear her purr...even if he'd had no right to do that.

Collapsing, he rolled to one side so he didn't crush her.

"That was, ahh..."

He waited. Shouldn't matter what she said, but it did.

She curved against him, accepting his unspoken suggestion to snuggle on his chest. Kurt dragged the sheet up to make sure she didn't catch a chill. Didn't take half a second to regret his impulsiveness. Now he couldn't see her.

Her toes brushed across his calf as she adjusted herself once more.

"Nice," she finally finished.

"Nice?" Stroking her hair, he luxuriated in the feel of her in his arms.

"Very nice," she amended. "Can we do it again?"

"Sure," he said. "In a while. A man needs time to recover. I could teach you a few things in the interim, though."

Her small hand pressed against his shoulder. "You mean there's more?"

"Lady, the learning's just beginning."

She smiled, softly, secretively. Wiggling one more time, Jessie rose on one elbow to look at him. Blasted sheet hadn't fallen away.

Her hair trailed down, onto his chest, feeling like satin ribbon...the way he'd imagined it would. Unable to help himself, he entwined its length between his fingers.

Possession walloped him. As unwelcome as it was unexpected, Kurt shoved away the feeling.

It stayed away precisely three seconds.

Making love to her had been a mistake. It complicated things tenfold. He intended to help her discover herself, see herself as an attractive woman.

He hadn't expected to find her irresistible himself. Hadn't expected that an odd sense of chivalry would want to keep her protected. He'd told her to find a man to love her and cherish her.

When she did, he figured he'd sink his fist into the nearest wall.

"Did it feel as good as you hoped?" she asked shyly.

"Hmm?"

"My hair, you know, on your chest."

"No."

She frowned.

"It felt better."

"Beast."

"Oh, yeah?" he asked, using his hold to draw her closer. "I'll show you how beastly." Not even a minute ago, he'd decided that making love with her was worse than a bad idea.

Now he intended to do it again.

Never figured that once he carried her upstairs, rational thought would stay behind.

Kurt was quickly learning that when it came to Jessie, the game had no rules. Number one problem with that was that he liked rules and boundaries.

Or he had. Until now.

Something sizzling sparked in his green eyes, making brandy-colored spikes appear. She shivered.

He was all man, large and overwhelming. She looked at him, drinking in the sight of dark hair matted on his chest, stretching across...and down.

She gulped.

Heaven help her, she didn't know if she could get enough of him.

The most secret part of her was warm, fulfilled, yet that inexplicable yearning returned even as she looked at Kurt. It was impossible to believe they'd actually made love, yet her body knew it beyond dispute.

She wanted to run her hands over him....

"Roll over onto your stomach," he said.

Kurt obviously had other plans for her.

"I'm going to discover how I need to touch you for you to cry out."

She'd asked for this, hadn't she?

Some of her shyness had vanished, but none of the trepidation. It still took total trust to give herself completely to a man when, before Kurt, she'd experienced nothing but hurt.

Instinctively she knew now that Kurt would never intentionally hurt her. It was the unintentional part that bothered her the most.

"Here." He offered a hand.

She accepted.

When she sat up, he pulled down the sheets, placing a pillow where her stomach would rest.

Courage fled.

If she did what he asked, she'd be helplessly exposed. Unable to see or anticipate, he was asking her to make herself completely vulnerable to him.

Still holding her by the hand, he waited. No sign of impatience ticked in his temple. He'd placed the ball in her court. If she said no, it was obvious he wouldn't push her.

Jessie squeezed his hand, communicating what she couldn't possibly say.

Gently he helped her to turn over. His pillow smelled of him, equally comforting and terrifying.

A shift on the mattress told her he'd moved, then his footsteps were muted by the braided rug on the floor. Finally a whisper of air around her said he stood there, looking at her.

Trepidation traced her spine when he adjusted the pillow beneath her midsection, raising her hips even more toward him.

He'd already told her he found her desirable, and he'd proven she was woman enough for him. So why the sudden fear?

Had to be from the unknown, she decided, trying to still the frenetic race of her heart.

Old beliefs, though, they still haunted. Sam told her no

man would want her, but Kurt didn't seem to be suffering, or at least she fervently prayed he wasn't just being kind.

Unnecessarily she closed her eyes, anticipation coiling. Time moved forward, and he hadn't done anything, hadn't said anything.

Jessie wondered if she'd survive the night....

When she'd asked him to teach her, show her, she'd thought she'd known what she was asking for. Now she knew she hadn't had a clue. Her meager experiences with Sam hadn't prepared her for the sensual assault of a man like Kurt.

He was a feast for the eyes, filling her vision. With soft words, he was a feast for her hearing. Then his kisses—they'd been a feast of taste. Until an hour ago, she'd believed that the act was all there was to it, yet—

She cried out.

Again, he lightly brushed his fingers between her thighs.

"Couldn't tell whether you liked that or not."

A flood of heat cascaded through her.

He did it again and she squirmed, her toes seeking and not finding stability.

"Did you like it?"

The mattress beneath her face drowned her reply and smothered her gasp.

"Jess?"

"Yes!" she confessed, turning her head to one side.

She imagined, rather than saw, his smile.

"And this?" He rubbed her feet.

Heaven, she thought, her toes curling.

Next he took her hair and moved it to the side, blindfolding her with it. Beast was right.

Moisture traced her earlobe.

Not knowing where he'd touch next made her squirm,

heightening every response in her body. She was aroused in places she didn't know it was possible to be aroused.

He drew a line down the middle of her back, then kept going until she whimpered.

"There?"

"No!"

"No?" he asked.

"Yes!"

"Ah."

Then his finger caressed her where he'd made love to her earlier. This time she screamed. Pushing her knees into the mattress, she sought more.

Kurt kissed her calf.

He'd brought her to awareness from her head to her toes, never lingering, only leaving a promise.

During her life, she'd learned never to anticipate any thing; it only led to disappointment. Yet right now, Kurt was undoing all of that. She waited, wondering where he'd roam next, and would it be with just his finger, or with his mouth?

He nipped the flesh of one of her buttocks, then laved away the tiny hurt.

"Seemed you liked this better," he murmured, trailing the blunted tip of a fingernail on the sensitive inside flesh of her left thigh.

She quivered. Against conscious will, her legs parted. He plumped the pillow, opening her more to his view.

The sound of his breath hung as a reassuring reality, but in truth, nothing about this seemed real.

He kissed her nape. She felt certain she'd go mad with the sensations that built, demanding release. "Kurt..."

"Tell me, Jessie. Tell me where you want me to touch you."

She couldn't.

"Then I'll have to figure it out." He took her left arm and drew it above her head.

Her fingers felt the solidness of the wooden headboard. Instinctively she reached for it, needing something to hang on to.

With strokes that could hardly be called a touch, he roamed over her shoulder, then down her side, her breasts swelling in hope. But he didn't linger, continuing down, over her ribs, the indentation of her waist, the flare of her hip, her thigh, calf, then he outlined her toes before starting back up the inside.

Her hips pushed off the pillow. One part of her knew what she was doing was more daring than anything she'd ever done, the other part didn't care, she simply *wanted*.

Instead of pausing at her apex as she'd known he would, he went up her back, then started over.

This time, he went a little faster. She wiggled and squirmed. He laughed softly.

"Tell me," he said.

Next time, when he caressed her *there*, she would...she swore. But she didn't. Her head tossed back and forth as that burning in her belly increased. Her nipples were hard and the friction of her movements made them ache. He'd formed his mouth around them earlier and she wanted it again. "Kurt..."

The rhythm built, fast, faster... Then he abruptly stopped.

She groaned into the mattress, wondering if his exquisite torture would kill her.

Leaning over her, he began to stroke her from the other side, using the same, maddening, arousing motions. Seconds later, he traced both sides of her body simultaneously, pausing at the sides of her breasts.

She lifted her body slightly, shamelessly, hoping that he'd reach beneath her to fondle her nipples.

But he seemed more content to drive her to the brink...

"Kurt, I want you, please." Need had banished embarrassment and suddenly she felt freer than she had her entire life.

He made a sound, somewhere between a growl and a promise. "Do you trust me?"

"Make love to me," she demanded.

He did.

Moving between her legs without rolling her onto her back, he slowly entered her, filling her, stretching her.

The feelings exquisite, she sobbed out his name.

Then he began to move.

Desperately she hung onto the headboard, then began to move in timing with him. He was...incredible.

He drove in deeper and she could no longer think, her head tossing from side to side.

Gently he kissed her neck and brilliant light flooded her vision, even though her eyes were completely closed.

She shattered totally.

Nothing like this had ever happened to her before. Yet slowly her befuddled mind comprehended that he wasn't done.

Heaven help her.

She pulled her lower lip between her teeth and absorbed the pulsing little shocks as her body accommodated him.

One of his hands circled her shoulder, his fingers biting into her.

Impossibly moisture began to build inside her again.

It couldn't happen again, so soon, she told herself. Could it?

"Jess..." Her name tore from his throat.

One thing was certain, she'd never again be the same woman she'd been when she asked Kurt to father her child.

But she wondered, would she be better, or would the experience destroy her?

Nine

Kurt prowled the kitchen, grabbing the ingredients to make omelettes. He was ravenous. But not necessarily for food.

The sound of the shower trickled down the stairs, like a siren's song. He told himself he could resist it, resist her.

He was wrong.

Turning off the burner, he strode up the stairs and into the bathroom.

Steam puffed over the shower door, fogging the window and leaving a haze in the air that reminded him of the effect she had on his brain.

He hadn't been this hot for a woman in years, if ever. He'd always enjoyed making love, but with Jessie...

He exhaled. She was incredible, responsive, daring. Her reaction drove him onward.

He'd married Belinda, believed himself to be totally and completely in love with her. Now he wondered. Yeah, her betrayal hurt, more than anything his pride stung. A woman who professed to love you didn't hop from one bed to another.

Kurt couldn't help but realize he intended for Jessie to do precisely that, leave his bed and find another man's, a man who wouldn't need to use a condom as he buried himself inside her. After all, she wanted a baby.

Something tightened inside him. He refused to name it as anger, but there it was, seething.

He didn't intend to get married. Belinda had cured him of the need for a golden lasso.

So why on earth was he standing here, tempting fate?

"Kurt?" She inched open the door, and just the simple sight of her face, compounded by the knowledge of what was still hidden, made him hard.

"Since you didn't come down for breakfast, thought I'd join you," he said.

Her eyebrows arched in surprise. "In here?"

He nodded.

"But...how, er, I mean..."

"Where there's a will..."

A slow smile slipped across her kissable lips.

"Is that a yes?" he asked.

In response, she pulled the door open another few inches. "Only if I get to watch you finish undressing."

He was barely wearing any clothes as it was. Jeans and briefs.

Water dripped down her, dropping onto her shoulders and chest, beading on her breasts before beginning another descent. This Jessie wasn't the woman he'd slung over his shoulder and brought into his home.

She'd blossomed, coming into her own, discovering latent sexuality, finding that she possessed strength and determination. He hoped she'd realized she was beautiful, as well, from the inside out.

Any man would be lucky to have her.

Why the hell did that thought stab, like a knife to his gut?

Maybe because she fit so perfectly in his arms. Or maybe because she made him want to be so much more than he was. Or maybe, just maybe, because his bed was empty, and until now, he hadn't noticed it was lonely, too.

Still, he steeled himself; she belonged to someone else, a man who would appreciate her, give her what she wanted and needed, someone who wasn't afraid of love, someone who didn't expect cheating at every turn.

That man wasn't him.

Even if a secret part of him wanted to be.

At the end of two more days, she'd be free, and he wouldn't look back. Maybe he'd even get an invite to the wedding.

That thought curdled his coffee.

"Kurt," she said huskily, "I'm waiting."

This was different, reaching for the top fastener of his jeans while she stared at him.

Just the sight of her had aroused him. The knowledge that she waited impatiently for him made it worse.

He ended up turning away to pull down the zipper the rest of the way.

"Spoilsport," she said, the soft sound of her laughter wrapping around him.

More steam clung to the warm air, a cloud billowing between them.

"I can't quite reach this spot in the middle of my back," she said as he finally walked toward her.

"It isn't your back I'm interested in this time."

"Oh."

Then he showed her exactly what he *was* interested in.

Minutes later, he triumphantly caught her body as she pitched forward, spent.

Holding her there felt right. Her head rested on his chest, her damp hair trailing across his body. Water ran over both of them, and for him, erased any feeling that he shouldn't be doing this.

There would be time later for regret. Right now, his only regret was that he was flesh and blood, not some super-human who could make love with her all day long.

He lost track of time, everything except the sound of her breathing, the sensual feel of her against him. But when she pulled away and slid one hand down him, reaching for him, closing her fingers around his hardness, the back of his head hit the ceramic tiles.

He dragged a breath through clenched teeth. Any sense of her shyness had vanished.

"Am I doing it right?" she asked, looking up at him through the long veil of lashes and sluicing water.

"You're doing..." He gulped down a groan along with the rest of his sentence.

She moved gently. Need gnawed at him, and Jessie seemed to sense it, moving in shorter, faster motions. His eyes closed as heat coiled and threatened to unravel.

"Kurt?"

He couldn't answer. Seconds later, he was lost.

When he finally recovered enough to look at her, she was grinning. He placed a kiss on the top of her head.

"Guess you liked it?"

"Yeah," he agreed. "Guess I did." What he didn't tell her was that no other woman had ever done that for him.

She was getting to him all right, under his skin and into his heart.

He knew he needed to end their relationship before he got in any deeper. Deep was for kids and men who didn't know their mind. He'd been there before. He didn't like it. Nope. It definitely wasn't for Kurt Majors.

Yet when she tongued away a trickle of moisture from his chin, he didn't stop her. Nor did he stop her when she reached for a bar of soap and looked at him questioningly.

And he sure as mountain snow didn't stop her when she worked up a lather, then started with his shoulders and worked her way downward.

Absently he wondered if she'd be the death of him.

If so, he might be the first man to die with a smile on his lips.

Jessie figured she could get used to being carried in his arms.

After gently drying her off, he carried her to his bed, then delivered firm instructions for her to stay put while he brought breakfast to her.

Feeling decadent—and liking it—she stayed put. After plumping the pillows and stacking them against the headboard, she reached for the flannel shirt he'd given her. It slipped over her shoulders, the well-worn cotton soft.

When he left the room, he'd taken the rest of her clothes, saying he was going to wash them. But the expression in his eyes told another story. The less she was wearing, the easier it would be to get her undressed.

That thought thrilled.

There wasn't a part of her body that didn't tingle from his exploration. He'd discovered every part of her, and just the memory of his discoveries made her cheeks burn.

She burrowed beneath the comforter, pulling it around her. A wet layer of spring snow had fallen last night, and ice frosted the bedroom windowpane. But the wind had stopped howling an hour ago and now weak rays of sunlight played on the glass, illuminating brilliant bursts of colorful ice crystals.

The world appeared perfect. For the first time in her life, she felt perfect, too. She wasn't emotionally cold and unresponsive. And a man—one in particular—seemed to delight in that exploration. On second thought, maybe she didn't need the comforter.

Smells of eggs and coffee drifted up the stairs, making her stomach growl. She'd been so filled with Kurt that she hadn't even noticed she was hungry.

There was something so intimate, so homey about being in his bed while he prepared her breakfast. Another first. A delicious sensation traced up her spine. She'd never been treated this way before.

A secret part of her never wanted it to end.

"Come and get it."

She glanced toward the door. Kurt carried a tray, laden with enough food for several days. Thankfully he had also brought coffee.

His eyes twinkled mischievously. He wore nothing other than blue jeans. And he expected her to eat when she couldn't even think straight.

"Well?" he prompted.

"I thought you wanted me here, in bed."

"Ah, but if you get up, I can undress you."

"I'm only wearing a shirt."

"Like I said, if you get up, I can undress you."

She gulped.

He came into the room, advancing purposefully.

"You can't be serious," she said, "about wanting me to eat breakfast without any clothes on."

He sighed. "Okay, okay, I'll let you eat first. You'll need your strength for when I strip you and take you back to bed."

She could barely force herself to eat.

Coffee cups were left half-full and plates half-empty. When he took her omelette away, she didn't protest. And when he unbuttoned her shirt, she reached for his jeans.

He made love to her. There was no other description. He brought her to awareness, allowed her to wobble on the precipice, then he caught her.

Minutes later, she lay in his arms, her head nestled on his shoulder, her hair sifting across his chest. With a motion that mimicked the beat of her heart, he stroked her arm, saying nothing.

She stayed there for a very long time, enjoying the quiet, pretending as if this moment might last forever, even though she knew it wouldn't, couldn't.

As she rode the rhythmic rise and fall of his chest, she quietly asked, "Kurt, do you believe in love?"

His hand stilled on her arm. "Love?"

She didn't respond.

"Yeah, guess I do."

She waited, wondering if he'd continue.

"I've seen my parents together for enough years. Gotta believe in it."

"But what about for you?"

"Used to."

"Until Belinda."

He was silent for so long, she was sure she'd overstepped imaginary boundaries.

"Until Belinda," he agreed. When he spoke, though, it was with an emotional burr in the words.

"Will you tell me about her?"

She inhaled his scent, soap and shower, spiced with the earthiness of spring. The way she rested on him—cradled by strength—offered her protection. He kept her warm, fed her fantasies.

To think, she'd been willing never to experience this kind of intimacy with a man...

His hand stopped moving on her arm. "Guess the relationship wasn't what she was looking for."

"Just like that?"

"It wasn't that simple. I was working with a new horse, Tarnation."

She laughed slightly, then he shifted their positions, drawing her up a little. Turning more on her side, she reached across him, placing her palm on his shoulder.

"Tarnation decided he was tired of training, so he dumped me in a pile of...mud, yeah, mud. I came in to change." When he continued, there was bitterness tempering the rage. "Found Belinda cozying up to one of my ranch hands."

Jessie's eyes squeezed shut. Even though the town was small, gossip had never supplied that detail, testimony to the fact Kurt was a gentleman. She'd heard the relationship hadn't worked out, nothing more. Even Miss Starr hadn't gotten more information than that. "Belinda did this in your house?" she asked, disbelievingly.

"In my bed."

Oh heavens. "I'm sorry," she said, knowing the words were inadequate.

"It was a long time ago."

But hurt didn't just go away because time had passed—how well she knew that.

"When I fired the hand, then turned on her, she apologized, but not until she figured I was going to send her away, too."

"Did you give her a second chance?"

"No."

His harshness echoed through her. She'd seen the caring side of Kurt, with his pregnant dog and at the center where they volunteered. He exemplified concern. Jessie had even been there when he fought for kids, intervening on their behalf to get them a second chance.

Right now, she wondered how well she really knew him.

"Love doesn't behave that way," he said. "She couldn't have loved me and done that."

"And your love for her died right then."

"In an instant."

Neither said anything and sunshine pushed through the frosted windowpanes, as if offering a promise of nature, of the future.

"Love cares," Kurt said. "It protects and puts someone else's feelings first. At least it should."

He'd seen that, in his parents' marriage. That was the only place she'd ever seen it also. But for Kurt it was different. He'd known the experience; she'd only enjoyed it vicariously.

"So you'll never get married again?" She waited.

"No."

Why the abrupt answer made her heart catch, she didn't know.

"What about you, Jessie?"

He began those wonderfully frustrating little motions again. It felt so right, so comfortable, so arousing...

"Will you get married?"

"I don't know," she confessed.

"Four days ago, you were sure you wouldn't."

"Four days ago, I didn't realize anyone might want to marry me."

"And now?"

Kurt drew her toward him, tangling his fingers in her hair.

Now, life was different, she realized. "I don't know," she confessed. "I don't know."

And then, no more words were spoken. They weren't needed.

Jessie hummed while she towel-dried her body.

The drag of nubs across her sensitized skin caused a memory of Kurt's touch to return. She smiled, forgetting the melody of the song she was trying to hum. Since she couldn't carry a tune anyway, she figured that was probably for the best.

The hem of one of his shirts hung across her thighs, and he'd offered her a pair of sweatpants to wear while her clothes were in the washer. Thankfully the sweats had a drawstring at the waist. She rolled up the bottoms several times. Makeshift clothing. But it didn't matter to her. Right at this moment, she was happier than she'd ever been.

A whole new world was opening for Jessie, one that offered glimpses of possibility and hope. Until Kurt, she'd believed that happily ever after didn't exist beyond the last page of a book.

But now...now she'd discovered she wasn't an ugly duckling. No man could make love to her like Kurt had and only pretend an interest.

He'd seen every inch of her, naked and in bright light. She had flaws, she knew them, had inventoried them on more than one occasion, yet they didn't seem to matter to Kurt.

In his arms, his bed, his shower, she felt beautiful. He'd given her so much—hope, trust, but most important, he'd offered her the chance to believe in herself.

He'd asked her earlier about marriage, and the question returned. Tightly gripping the ends of the towel, she dared to dream...imagining a man truly being interested in fathering her child...her breath caught...imagining a man loving her, cherishing her, letting her become part of a real family for the first time in her life.

Thanks to Kurt, she dared to think that there might be someone out there for her, a man who knew her faults and loved her anyway, a man who was patient, understanding, a man who would teach her, a man like...

Jessie dug her fingers into the towel and pushed away the thought before it fully formed. She couldn't allow herself to take it any further.

Squeezing her eyes shut, she told herself she couldn't think of him in those terms. He was her best friend's brother, *her friend,* nothing more.

Sure, her heart whispered.

Every time Jessie had listened to her heart, she'd been hurt. She thought Sam was the right man for her. She'd believed some family, somewhere, someday, would want to keep her.

She couldn't even consider Kurt as a candidate for anything more than a sperm donor. When he'd refused her, he'd eliminated that possibility. Now there was nothing between her and Kurt except friendship.

She wondered why that was suddenly a harder truth to swallow than Sam's rejection had been.

With determination, she pushed away the sting of her musings, deciding to allow herself only to concentrate on the happiness she was feeling. Fluffing her hair, she went in search of Kurt.

He'd promised conversation and coffee after he'd finished his chores. Their time together would end soon and she didn't want to waste a minute of it.

"Happy birthday to you, happy birthday to you! Happy birthday, dear Jessie...happy birthday to you!"

Her eyebrows drawn together, she went downstairs, following the sound of Kurt's voice into the kitchen. Sunshine lay on the floor, her puppies scrabbling all over her. And Kurt was standing near the table, grinning.

He held a badly, very badly, wrapped present in one hand. A cake sat on the table, decorated with her name and sporting—she was sure—far too many candles. He'd blown up balloons and scattered them around the kitchen. "Surprise!"

"*Ahhh....*"

"Since you never had a party, I thought I'd throw you a surprise one."

She broke into a smile that encompassed all the radiance of her heart. "It's not my birthday."

"How do you know?"

"Well, they found me in summer."

"But you didn't have a birth certificate."

Emotion stung her eyes. She'd never had anyone care for her like this...never.

"The birthday girl deserves a kiss."

He slowly moved toward her, popping a balloon and scaring a yelp out of Sunshine and the puppies.

"Isn't there something about a spanking for each year, too?" he teased, taking her in his arms.

"You wouldn't!"

"Maybe later."

Then all thought vanished as he drew her hips against him and she felt his hardness. Kurt lay claim to a kiss, one that explored her entire mouth and shot little sensations from her mind to her womb.

When he finally ended it, encouraging her to open her present, she needed to sit down. Her legs would no longer support her.

Eagerly she tore the gift wrap, unveiling a stuffed teddy bear. "Oh, Kurt."

"I remembered that you had a teddy bear growing up," he said, the words emerging awkward and stilted.

She clutched the tiny treasure to her chest, fighting tears. Nothing she'd ever received meant as much to her as thi bear. Looking at Kurt through a fringe of tears, wondering how she would ever repay these memories.

In amazement at his consideration, his caring, she shook her head. "Thank you," she whispered around the lump clogging her throat.

"It wasn't anything."

"To me, it is."

"Then you're welcome," he said, giving a smile tha melted her heart.

Grabbing a chair and turning it backward, he sat, watch ing her.

"I can't believe you did all this for me."

"I wanted to."

"But…" She trailed off as realization dawned. "You bought all these things yesterday, while you were in town." While she'd been pacing the house, fuming that he didn' care, getting angrier and angrier because she thought th only thing he was interested in was proving a point.

Why was it that, where he was concerned, she kept mak ing a fool out of herself?

"Cake?" he offered.

"Chocolate?"

"Is there any other kind?"

She took down two plates and found napkins, a knif and two forks, then returned to the table. She cut the slice and offered him the first.

"I'll feed you," he said.

"Feed me?" she squeaked.

He picked up one fork, stabbed it through a piece tha would never fit in her mouth, then told her, "Open up."

Gamely she did. Biting through the cake, she left half of it on the fork. *"Ohhh,"* she murmured. She'd never tasted anything so rich, so sweet.

Turning the fork back toward him, Kurt helped himself to the uneaten part.

A dribble of icing remained near his lip, and without thinking, she reached for it.

Kurt caught her hand before she could wipe the frosting on a napkin. He closed his mouth around her finger and sucked on it deeply.

She all but slithered deeper into her chair.

"Another bite?" he asked.

"I... Yes."

His grin tantalized. Instead of pushing the fork's prongs through the cake, he used his index finger to scoop icing from the top.

"Open wide."

She did. This time, she suckled his finger, curling her tongue and working it around to lick all the sweetness from him.

Because of the way he sat, she saw his reaction, welcomed it. He wasn't immune to her and knowing that was as heady as the impromptu birthday party.

"We'll finish the cake later," he said, his voice rolling with a husk.

She couldn't think of anything better....

Jessie Stephens was getting to him.

Minute by minute, she was getting under his skin, angling closer to his heart.

He didn't know when it happened or why he'd allowed it to happen. But the fact was, he cared for Jessie. It wasn't in the same way it had been a few days ago, before they'd made love, before she'd taught him a few things.

Her teaching him hadn't been part of the bargain.

He'd been on a mission to show her that her thinking was wrong, that she couldn't be a one-man army, and most of all, that she wasn't the unattractive woman she believed.

He'd ended up discovering she was undeniably attractive, that her beauty came from the inside and radiated outward, that if anyone had the heart to truly love, it was Jessie.

Pausing, he put a booted foot on the head of the shovel. Across the barn, Lasso tipped his head and neighed demandingly. "Be right there," Kurt promised. Anything to distract himself from the thought of the woman he'd left in his shower. Naked and wet in his shower, his mind amended.

Didn't matter that the temperature hovered somewhere just above freezing; he wiped a damp brow. Yeah, she was getting to him. Even out here in the cold, he couldn't escape thoughts of her warmth.

After they'd made love, he'd escaped. Hadn't been a better word for it than that. Something unsettling roiled in his gut, and he'd had to get away from it, exorcize it with physical labor.

Only problem was, it wasn't working.

He couldn't get her out of his mind.

Kurt didn't have the right to be thinking about her. That right belonged to another man, one who would be able to offer her love and trust.

With renewed vigor, he resumed cleaning the stall.

Kurt found another dozen or so chores to kill the next hour. He wanted her fully dressed when he went into the house. All he needed to do was look at her and he wanted to take her back to bed. And that, he knew, was dangerous territory.

Finally reaching the back door, he paused, watching her.

She was on her knees, petting Sunshine and fussing over the puppies, particularly the one he'd given her. She'd named it Rocky, like the mountains, saying the pup was going to grow up big and strong. He'd told her to dream big...she'd said she always did.

And now, so was he. For a second, while he allowed the fantasy to play out, he imagined coming home every evening, after a long hard day on the range, to this scene, a lovely woman in his house, someone to love him and care for him.

That soon shattered, though, with the memory of Belinda and the homecoming he had experienced.

Loneliness had its rewards.

It was without betrayal.

As if sensing his presence, Jessie glanced up. Her smile was inviting, and it was directed at him.

He felt as though he'd been branded with his own iron.

"Sorry. Didn't hear you come in."

His arms wanted to hold her, his hands wanted to be buried in her hair as he pulled her closer.

"Want some coffee, maybe something to eat?"

The scent of soap and shampoo lingered in the air. His clothes hung on her, but they couldn't disguise her feminine curves. He wanted, again, already.

"Kurt?"

He reminded himself he shouldn't continue to make love to her, especially now that he realized he was starting to care for her.

"Lunch would be great."

She frowned a little, her palm stilling on Sunshine's head. "Everything okay?"

Hadn't been since he'd tossed her over his shoulder and carried her into his house. His mind had been first to go. Sanity soon followed. "Sure."

Her frown didn't fade, but she stood. "You made breakfast. I'll make lunch."

After excusing himself, he went into the bathroom to wash up.

When he returned, she was washing dishes and the newspaper she'd brought in caught his eye. Turning to page three for Miss Starr's column, his eyelids narrowed.

Jessie's name leaped out, along with his. He formed a fist as he read.

I promised I would deliver the latest news when it came to Jessica Stephens knitting baby booties. Miss Starr never disappoints! And so, loyal readers, here's the scoop. Take a deep breath....

While I can't say for sure that Jessica Stephens is pregnant—after all, I would hate to spread untruths—it appears that if she is, it would be by none other than Kurt Majors!

Kurt Majors, that's right.

It seems Kurt kidnapped the young lady, tossing her over his shoulder, right in front of the neighbors. Mrs. Johnson said she'd never seen anything like it in all her born years.

Mercy, it's almost enough to make a grown woman swoon. Imagine, being kidnapped by a handsome young man demanding marriage....

Kurt was in town yesterday buying a stuffed animal at the gift store. One can't help but wonder if it might be for a baby! When asked about Jessica, he reportedly didn't deny the kidnapping or the fact he was still holding Jessica captive.

Well, if and when a wedding date is announced, you can depend on me to bring you the information right away. After all, Miss Starr considers it her duty to keep you informed.

For now, this is all the news you can use. Oh, my, are those wedding bells I'm hearing?

Kurt dragged a hand through his hair.

He waited a few seconds for the anger to hit.

It didn't.

Surprisingly the column didn't upset him, even though he expected it to. His parents, and especially Mary, would be none-too-pleased with his Neanderthal behavior. He wouldn't blame them if they were upset. He could take the heat, though.

Jessie, on the other hand, would be mortified by the column. And the speculation sure complicated things for her if she decided to go ahead with having another man father her child.

The thought of another man bedding her caused a slip-knot to cinch in his gut.

He pictured her, walking into the post office or general store, everyone imagining that the baby she carried was his and whispering that he hadn't fulfilled his duty to her.

By damn, he wouldn't tolerate it.

He knew enough about her already to know that she would continue to defy his wishes. If he let her get away, she would find a man—*a donor,* probably anonymous. She still had an appointment scheduled and that nagged him, like a burr caught between denim and skin.

She wanted a baby. But he didn't want her sleeping with any other man, or worse, collecting a specimen and having it medically placed.

Simple as that.

Love didn't enter into it. Then again, did that really matter? He'd loved Belinda and that had bought him a pickup load of troubles.

He and Jessie would be a good match. He liked kids, wouldn't mind having someone to pass the ranch on to. Jessie was strong, loyal, determined. She knew his business as well as he did. She'd be a good asset in that area.

And she sure was sweet in his bed...

Getting her pregnant wouldn't be a hardship.

And next winter wouldn't be as long and lonely with Jessie beneath his covers.

The thought of Jessie as his wife appealed to every one of his senses.

Before he talked himself out of it, he said, "Jessie?"

"Hmm?" She turned to face him, soap bubbles clinging to her hands.

Her smile captivated him. The way the sun shone through the window and played on the golden highlights in her hair made him recall the darkness of it earlier, when it had still been wet from their shared shower.

She dried her hands, dropped the towel on the counter, then drew her eyebrows together quizzically.

After he'd kidnapped her, she'd been in an impossible situation and made the most of it. He'd seen her patience and determination with the kids at the center, seen her dedication to her work when she did his books and discussed moneymaking strategies. She had looks and brains. The perfect combination.

Yeah, she'd make a good wife.

Why hadn't he seen this as the perfect answer days ago?

Strangely, though, when he tried to ask her the most important question he could imagine, words seemed to stick in his throat. He finally pulled them out, only to discover they were husky and resonated with rawness. "Jessie, will you marry me?"

Ten

Marry him?

Jessie's knees threatened to buckle.

This was the moment she'd wanted her whole life, dreamed of, anticipated.

And it was the moment she'd never believed would happen to her.

She clenched her hands at her sides, hoping the dig of her fingernails served the same purpose as pinching herself. "Marry you?"

He grinned, closing the distance. His boots echoed on the scarred vinyl floor, each sound intensified against the pulse sounding in her ears.

Stopping barely a foot from her, Kurt placed his hands around her, holding her tight. Jessie wanted to believe, desperately, but this was so unexpected, so incredible.

"Yes, marry me. As in a wedding, a ring, a dress, a baby."

She looked at him, searching for any sign he was kidding, that this was nothing more than a cruel joke like the one Sam had pulled. But she found nothing there, except seriousness. Even his grin had faded. "A..." She sucked in a searing breath. "Baby?"

"Maybe a couple. Brothers and sisters are good."

"But...why?"

His brows drew together. "Why?"

"Why would you want to marry me? I mean, you could have any woman..." Color crept up her face. "Any woman you wanted."

He shook his head. "I don't want any woman. I want you."

"Kurt..."

His grip on her shoulders tightened intently.

"I thought we'd established that you're attractive."

His gaze swept down her, slowly, as if he was mentally recording every detail. For a second or two, he lingered at her breasts.

Just when she thought she couldn't take anymore, her body responding to the mere suggestion of everything they'd shared, he met her eyes again.

"I could give you a reminder if you wanted."

She wondered if the color in her cheeks would permanently stain. "No."

"Too bad. All I have to do is hold you, Jessie, and I'm ready again."

His suggestive words sent a flood of warmth cascading through her.

"It'd be nice to have a son or daughter to pass the ranch on to. You want a baby. It's the perfect solution."

"But you said you'd never marry again."

"Jessie—"

She tried again, "But—"

"You're the right wife for me, Jessie. We're good together sexually."

Even the roots of her hair must be turning color, she was sure.

"Getting you pregnant would be a pleasure."

She couldn't take any more...Jessie uncurled her fists.

"Skin to naked skin," he said.

His hold on her didn't allow her to look away. She thought of the possibilities, of her belly swelling with his baby, a child conceived the natural way, not at a doctor's office or with perfunctory lovemaking, but as a result of a real marriage.

Her innermost dreams coalesced. Oh, she'd never ached like this, so deep in her womb.

His thumb meandered up and down the column of her throat. "You're strong, Jessie, caring, a good businesswoman. What more could a man want from the woman he asks to be his wife?"

Hope flickered, flaring inside her, filling her. She was so excited she could barely breathe. To have someone hold her on long winter nights, to care for her, to make love to her and start a family...a man like Kurt to wipe her brow when she was in labor, then snuggle a tiny infant in his large arms...it was the stuff of dreams—secret dreams she'd never shared for fear of jinxing them.

Instinct, though, born from so many years of rejection, urged caution. She wanted to shove the fear away and say yes to his proposal and be his bride.

But...

He hadn't mentioned love. He'd said earlier that he no longer believed in love. Surely, though, he must feel something to ask her to marry him. Surely...

She searched his eyes, reading nothing in their enigmatic depths.

She was torn, confused.

"I need to think," she said, pulling away from him, even though that was the last thing her heart wanted to do.

He let her go. She didn't know whether or not to be glad.

Kurt leaned against the sink where she'd been washing the cutting board and knives. She paced the confines of the kitchen, sensing that if she left the room, he'd follow her.

He wanted an answer, and she'd learned over the last few days that a determined Kurt was a dangerous man.

The open newspaper caught her eye. As if it were in large, bold print, her name leaped out.

Her heart momentarily stopped.

"Jessie, don't."

Kurt crossed to her, placing a hand on her shoulder. She shoved it away and picked up the paper, reading every solitary, painful word.

Tears of hopelessness welled in her eyes. She tried to blink away the burning moisture, only to have it fall, running down her cheeks.

All her hopes died in that instant.

Happily ever after may exist for some people. Not for her. Not ever for her. She should have known that. *She should have known.*

"You were wrong about chivalry, Kurt, it's not dead." She fought for bravery, only to have it slip away like a feather gulped by the wind.

"Thanks for the offer, but life taught me that I don't need a knight in shining armor." The lie stung her lips. She did need a knight in shining armor. Kurt just wasn't it.

She couldn't live her life knowing that pity made him propose to her, she couldn't. Living without love was one thing, being pitied was another.

Praying she wouldn't crumple, she reached unseeingly for his keys and grabbed them from the table.

Then, barely holding herself together, she ran.

"Damn it, Jessie! Wait."

She didn't.

"You don't understand, Jessie."

She understood, all right. All too well. He'd proposed to her because he had no other choice, not because he wanted to. He didn't want a wife. He didn't want *her*.

Fumbling with the doorknob and muttering an unintelligible curse, she finally freed the lock and hurried to his pickup truck, shoving the key into the ignition and cranking it until the engine roared to life.

Seeing Kurt right behind her, she locked the door and floored the accelerator, tears blurring in keeping with the mud splattering behind her.

She didn't pause at the end of the driveway, afraid he'd catch up to her.

Always a gentleman, he would have thought he ruined her reputation. Well, he hadn't. She swiped at her eyes with her fingertips and fought to take a breath.

She'd lived in this town her entire life, endured taunting as a child, had never been wanted or needed, had been rejected and now... Only slowing for a stop sign, she took off again, desperate to get home. She would survive a ruined reputation; she'd survived worse. Or at least that's what she tried to tell herself.

There was no doubt she'd asked an honorable man to father her baby.

He wouldn't have walked out on her if he'd agreed. But he wouldn't have ever loved her, either.

Outside her house, she collapsed against the steering wheel.

Jessie had never hurt this bad in her entire life, not when

they'd taken away her teddy bear, not when the Smiths said they didn't want to adopt her, not even when Sam said he wasn't interested in her. Never.

Maybe it was because until now, she'd never offered her own love.

But, with the clarity that often came from pain, she realized she loved Kurt.

Oh, heavens. How had it happened? When?

She didn't want to love Kurt. Any time she'd allowed herself to care, she'd been hurt. This time was obviously no exception. She shuddered, gripping the steering wheel tighter.

And she saw Mrs. Johnson looking out her window, a witness to Jessie's numbing pain.

That no longer mattered, though. She ached.

The tears fell in earnest as her heart broke.

Kurt cursed himself. He was a fool. The worst kind. Only an idiot would have allowed her to get away. In his only vehicle.

He had no way to go after her, no way to explain.

The air bit through his shirt and he turned back toward the house. He'd tried to stop her. He'd failed.

He pounded his fist against the door frame. Didn't help. So he did it again.

Back inside, Sunshine lifted her head and whined.

"I know," Kurt said, but then wondered, did he? He obviously didn't know a whole lot.

Finally, closing the front door on the spring's chill, he noticed that the ranch house rang with emptiness. The scent of her still lingered in the air. Remnant moisture from one of her tears still dusted his fingertip. He'd caused those tears with his arrogant assumption that she would marry him.

He should have known better.

Jessie had strength, lots of it. But when it came to her own interests, she was still fragile. He'd tried to prove, beyond a doubt, that she was attractive. That wasn't difficult.

The minute he'd unfastened the top button on her blouse, the first night when she'd asked him to father her baby, he'd desired her. He'd wanted her bare before him and he wanted to taste, to feel, to explore.

When it came to her emotions, though, he didn't have much experience. Maybe he should have learned something from his marriage. Obviously he hadn't.

Jessie probably believed him that she wasn't an ugly duckling, but would she believe that he wanted her, Jessie the person?

Damn it.

She was more important than the air he breathed. He needed her.

Striding to the phone, he grabbed the receiver and punched in her number. After the fourth ring, the answering machine clicked on.

He slammed down the receiver, refusing to spill his guts to a damn cassette tape.

Sunshine whined again, slapping her tail on the floor.

Kurt looked at his watch, calculating the amount of time it should take her to arrive home. Three minutes ago, he figured. Then, fighting for restraint, he decided he'd generously give her another five minutes, then try again.

And if she refused to answer...

Kurt refused to contemplate the possibilities. One way or another, he'd talk to her, make her see things his way. Make her see reason.

He might have been a fool once. Wouldn't happen again.

* * *

After grabbing her spare house key from under the Welcome mat, Jessie let herself in and drew the curtains against Mrs. Johnson's prying eyes. The woman had already seen enough, though, before Jessie managed to pull herself together. She'd probably be the topic of Miss Starr's next column, too.

She shuddered.

The phone rang and the illusion of being pulled together shattered.

Could it be Kurt?

And what would he say if it was? More, what would *she* say?

She let the answering machine take the call.

Hearing a woman's voice, Jessie's heart thundered to a stop. Of course it wasn't Kurt. Unless, of course, he wanted his truck back.

The woman caller said she wanted to confirm Jessie's appointment at the clinic.

Jessie collapsed against the wall and slid down it, sitting on the floor with one arm wrapped around her legs. She placed her other palm across her stomach.

Having a baby of her own had been her goal for months. She'd focused her whole life around it. She'd knitted baby booties, bought parenting magazines, even drawn sketches of the nursery.

Now she realized that she no longer wanted to be a single mother.

Kurt had been right all along.

Now that she'd had a taste of love, she knew how potent it was.

Children deserved it every bit as much as adults did. More than that, kids needed two parents, people who loved each other as much as they loved their kids. They needed

ome and hearth. They needed families. Most of all, they
eeded to know who their parents really were.

She'd gone through life not knowing, always wondering.
No birth certificate, no birthdays, always being an outsider
on holidays, no family reunions. It wouldn't have been exactly the same for her child—she would have made sure of
that—and yet, there'd be an uncertainty about the missing
daddy.

As much as she wanted a child, Kurt had made Jessie
realize she was no longer capable of going through with an
anonymous donation.

When the phone rang again, she buried her face in her
hands and cried for yet another broken dream.

Sunshine whined, thumping her tail, obviously wanting
to offer Kurt some comfort, but since she was busy with
her new puppies, Kurt went to her. Crouching to scratch
behind her ears, Kurt asked, "So what do I do now?"

He couldn't let Jessie vanish from his life.

Damn it, she shouldn't have left before he'd had the
chance to tell her he loved her.

Loved her?

Loved her?

The realization struck like a blow to the midsection.

He loved Jessie?

That wasn't possible.

She was his bookkeeper, his sister's lifelong friend, his
friend. Over the past few days, Jessie had become his lover,
but nothing more. The fact that they'd slept together meant
nothing.

Like hell.

He stood and Sunshine scrambled up beside him, looking
up at Kurt with dark, questioning eyes.

Pacing the room, he finally stopped in front of the win-

dow. A ray of sunshine slithered through the glass and int○
him, warming him.

He loved Jessie.

Like a lightning bolt striking the peak of a fourteer○
thousand-foot mountain, the knowledge illuminated even a○
it seared. Yeah, he loved her.

It wasn't expected, he hadn't seen it coming, he hadn'○
had time to duck.

After Belinda, falling in love had never been part of th○
plan.

Women were dishonest. He'd known that fact all the wa○
to his soul.

But Jessie had never been deceptive. She'd asked fo○
what she wanted, even though embarrassment threatened t○
devour her.

Women couldn't be trusted. He'd learned that the har○
way.

But Jessie had been a virgin when she came to him. Sh○
didn't give herself easily or lightly. The only other ma○
she'd nearly had sex with had been the man she was en○
gaged to.

Women cared about no one but themselves. He'd see○
that over and over with Belinda.

But Jessie volunteered at the children's center.

Women weren't capable of love.

But Jessie had looked at him earlier, with the same ex○
pression his mother still wore when she looked at his father○

Women were trouble.

And there, Jessie was no exception.

She'd waltzed in with wistful eyes and a healing touch○
She'd wanted him to teach her a few things. And he'd bee○
the student. She'd taught him to care, made his heart ope○
up again. Where there were wounds, now there was caring○

He placed his open hand on the window, the warmth○

welcoming. He recalled the feel of Jessie against him, the perfect way she fit in his arms. He recollected her vulnerability, her openness.

The breath he inhaled shook his lungs.

They'd connected emotionally, and that realization nearly brought him to his knees.

He wanted her. He needed her. He loved her.

Damn it all.

Her determination to have a family tortured him, like a searing brand to his insides. Earlier, he'd decided he didn't like the idea of her becoming pregnant by a donor. But what if she took him at his word and decided to find another man—damn it to hell—*someone Kurt was likely to know.*

The thought of another man tasting her, touching her, exploring her, possessing her, burned like hot metal at the back of his throat.

She deserved the family she wanted, but he would watch her body grow and change with his child...the baby resulting from their lovemaking.

Determination driving him, he snatched up the phone to call for a ride, gossip be damned. There were a few things that needed to be settled between him and Jessie. And settle them he would. Once and for all.

He called on Nick, his closest friend. They pretty well took turns helping each other out. He'd saved Nick's sorry butt down at the Wooden Nickel Saloon. Nick had still been nursing the wounds Marcy left on her way out of his life, and when trouble started... Nick had been spoiling for a fight.

Kurt had shuffled Nick out less than a minute before Spencer McCall had arrived, lights flashing, and none too happy about being dragged from bed. Now, Kurt figured it was his turn to collect.

Fifteen minutes later—fifteen interminably long minutes—Nick honked his horn.

"Where's your pickup?" Nick asked when Kurt had slammed the door.

"Jessie's house." Kurt's flat answer didn't invite further comment.

Nick never had learned to take a hint. "Jessie Stephens?"

"Yeah," he grumbled.

"She ran away in your vehicle?"

Kurt drummed his fingers on the dash, ignoring Nick's grin.

"Guess the little lady can take care of herself."

Kurt quirked a brow.

"Heard about the kidnapping this morning down at the Chuckwagon Diner. Didn't believe the rumor until now."

"This heap of junk go any faster?"

"Guess we're heading to Jessie's house, huh?"

"Anyone ever tell you you talk too damn much?"

Nick grinned again.

"Your turn's coming, buddy," Kurt said with an imminent sense of satisfaction. "There's going to be a woman who'll knock you from behind."

"Nah. Marcy already did that. Once was enough, thanks." He drove for a few minutes in silence. "This mean you're gonna make an honest woman out of Jessie?"

Kurt exhaled. "If she'll have me," he finally said. The fear that she wouldn't made his soul quake.

Following the directions Kurt provided, Nick stopped in front of Jessie's house.

"Good luck," Nick said, no trace of teasing, only support etched in the set of his shoulders.

"Thanks." Kurt reckoned he'd need it. He'd hurt her, made her wonder if she was truly as beautiful as he wanted her to believe. He'd been a fool. He'd never been much good at expressing his emotions. Now, he had no choice.

He wondered if the chill down his spine was from terror.

"If you're looking for a best man..."

"Thanks for the offer." Kurt grinned, then it faded.

Nothing in his life had ever meant as much as the next few minutes.

He exhaled with relief when he saw his truck parked out front. She hadn't left for Denver. Yet.

He slammed the pickup door closed and strode to the front porch. After Nick peeled away from the curb, Kurt knocked.

Thirty seconds later, he knocked again.

The third time, he pounded.

And she didn't answer, leaving Kurt to wonder just what the hell he was going to do next.

Eleven

Jessie was still sitting on the floor when she heard the knocking. She hugged herself as tears chased down her cheeks. No matter how hard she tried, she couldn't ignore the incessant pounding on the front door.

"Jessie, damn it, I know you're in there!"

Kurt.

She let out a shaky breath. Now what?

"Open up!"

She didn't move from her position on the floor.

"We need to talk."

By now, surely Mrs. Johnson had heard him. It wouldn't surprise Jessie to know that the entire neighborhood was watching Kurt. But after all she'd been through, this was only a minor embarrassment.

The pounding on the door stopped, only to have the hammering of her heart replace it.

She was surprised he'd given up this easily. It only went to show—

Jessie jumped.

The lock clicked open, followed immediately by the sound of the front door slamming.

She gulped.

Kurt stood there, his frame filling the doorway, blocking out the sunshine that had streamed in ahead of him.

"I asked you to open up."

"Kurt," she said breathlessly, wrapping her hands more securely around her, as if that could fend off the fear biting at her insides.

"I still had your keys."

He took a step toward her. She tried to shrink farther into the wall.

"You didn't answer my call."

She fought to show a calm her insides were nowhere close to feeling. "You said everything that needed to be said while we were at your house."

He scowled. "Don't kid yourself, lady."

His tone, cold and harsh, increased those tremors of fear. "What do you want from me?" she whispered. "I was going to return your truck tomorrow."

"I'm not interested in the truck."

He took another step, and her nerves jangled.

In seconds, he loomed over her and she was sorry she hadn't stood up before. If she did now, their bodies would touch, and she would come completely undone.

Even with the distance between them, she felt her body's betrayal. How did he manage to do that to her?

"Only thing I'm interested in is you, Jessie. You and me and that baby you want."

She shook her head. "I...I changed my mind." Closing her eyes, Jessie allowed her head to fall forward.

"You did what?"

Determinedly she wiped tears from her face. "You were right," she softly said, finding the courage to look at him. "I don't want to be a single parent, to raise a baby alone without support."

"You'll be a good mother, Jessie."

"Maybe. But I may never find out."

Coming closer, Kurt crouched in front of her. Face-to-face with him, her heart hurt. He was the man she loved and she wanted to touch him, feel the contours of his face and run her fingers through the thickness of his dark hair.

She longed to see his eyes lighten with the fire of exploration as they had when they'd made love. Instead a curtain of dark intensity shrouded his eyes. This wasn't the man who'd taught her so much; this Kurt was a stranger.

She wanted the past back.

"You will have that opportunity."

"So you've told me." She tried for an air of lightness. She failed. The words fell emotionless and empty into the thick tension permeating the living room. Being this close to the man she loved, knowing her feelings weren't returned, made her heart hurt.

"I'm going to be the father of your baby."

"You?"

"That's what you wanted, isn't it?"

So close… A few days ago, that would have been exactly what she wanted, but not now…now it wasn't nearly enough. The idea of sharing his bed, trying to make a baby while hiding her love would be asking the impossible.

The less she had to do with Kurt, the better. That was the only possible way to save the tattered remnants of her sanity. Yet that thought hurt so much more than she'd imagined it would. In losing Kurt, she'd lose years of friendship along with the fact that he looked out for her.

"Isn't that what you wanted, Jessie?" he repeated, his voice urgent. "For me to give you a child?"

"Not anymore. I want someone to share my life with, someone who'll love me as much as our baby."

He framed her face with his hands. "I am that man."

Her heart stammered, then stalled.

"I don't want any misunderstandings about what I'm saying, Jessie. I love you. I'm going to marry you and I'm going to be the father of our children."

"L-love?" The word froze in her throat. "It's just not, not possible."

"Love," he repeated. "And yeah, it is possible."

"But—"

"I'm not just saying it," he interrupted. "You're beautiful, from the top of your head, to the honesty in your eyes, the smile on your lips…" His gaze meandered downward. "To the way your breasts fit in my hands, the way your hips cradle me and the sexy pink on your toenails."

She couldn't look away if she wanted.

"You're a caring, compassionate woman. You'll be a great mother, a fantastic wife. Any man would be lucky to have you.

"I just want that man to be me."

She could barely breathe.

"I love you, Jessie. Asking you to marry me wasn't a joke, or something done out of pity. It came from my heart. I didn't see that, didn't say that before. Now I am. With my heart and soul, I want to marry you."

She searched his face, seeing that his eyes were even darker than before. And only then did she realize that their darkness revealed more than they concealed.

His hold on her face tightened and she saw the way his shoulders had bunched with tension. Her answer mattered to him…she mattered to him.

"Tell me you love me, too, Jessie. Tell me."

"Yes," she managed to say, her eyes swimming again with tears of joy instead of pain. "Yes, I love you."

He didn't smile, in fact lines were etched even more deeply beside his eyes.

Then, his voice husky and humble, he asked, "Will you do me the honor of becoming my wife?"

The honor was hers. "Yes," she whispered. "Yes, Kurt, yes."

"Jessie, what you do to me..." He claimed her mouth in a kiss of possession, demanding her surrender. She met it, exploring her own power over him, knowing her dreams had never, ever been this wonderful.

Finally pulling his lips from hers, he stood, drawing her to her feet, then against him. Rising onto her tiptoes, she wrapped her arms around his neck.

She sighed with contentment when he swept her from her feet and moved in the direction of her bedroom.

Before he placed her on the bed, he quietly asked, "Don't mind if we skip the protection this time, do you?"

The idea of Kurt buried inside her, their culmination maybe creating life, made her womb tighten. "No."

"Good. I want to feel you, all of you."

Then, starting with the top button of the shirt she wore, she gladly surrendered to him and their future.

Columbine Crossing Courier
"Around the Town" by Miss Starr

Miss Starr is delighted to be the first to bring you all the news you can use!

Kurt Majors has announced his engagement to Miss Jessica Stephens, and they're inviting the entire town to the wedding!

Jessica will become Mrs. Majors in less than two weeks. Rumor has it that he said he's not giving her a chance to change her mind. Oh, it does make Miss Starr's heart go pitter-patter...or, is that pitter-patter really the sound of little feet?

I promise, the instant I know anything about the due date of the Major production, you'll all be the first to know!

Until next week, this is all the news you can use. Oh, yes, except for the fact that our very own bridal shop will be providing Jessica's gown, reportedly a cowgirl confection of satin and lace.

See you there!

Miss Starr smiled. Mercy, she'd been waiting far too long to wear a pretty dress and white gloves. A wedding. Finally. And that she'd had a small hand in it made her stooped shoulders pull back with pride. Love made one young, didn't it?

From her post at the window, she saw Trudy leave the beauty shop and pause outside Henry's Snips and Clips, the stripes of the barber's pole going round and round, much like the repetition of Henry asking Trudy out and her turning him down.

Now, Miss Starr just needed to find a way to convince Trudy that she wasn't getting any younger. Goodness gracious, no one was! Trudy needed to learn that loneliness didn't pay any dividends.

And wonderful Lillian had brought in a lovely bouquet of flowers along with another book for her to read. This time it was about King Arthur and Guinevere. What was it about that dear child? Seemed the only stories she was interested in were ones with tragic endings. Miss Starr sighed.

There had to be someone out there for Lillian...there simply had to be.

It was springtime, after all, and a man's fancy turned to love. Or it did, as long as it had a little help. And that was precisely what Miss Starr had been born for.

Returning to her lookout station behind the counter, she carefully cut out the newspaper article and filed it.

Epilogue

"That husband of yours never told me I'd have to wear a tuxedo in order to get into your wedding," Nick grumbled good-naturedly.

"Sorry, Nick." Jessie smiled at their best man.

Effortlessly he moved across the dance floor with her, while Kurt danced with Lillian Baldwin. He'd seen Lillian standing in the corner, a lonely smile on her face. Kurt announced that no one should attend a reception without dancing. When Nick had claimed Jessie for a dance, Kurt had headed for Lillian.

Jessie knew her husband was an incredible man.

Her husband.

Her mind reeling with the impossibility of it all, she missed a step, only to have Nick effortlessly steady her, moving his hand instinctively lower on her back and smiling as if she'd never danced more perfectly.

She wondered if others saw the pain that darkened Nick's

blue eyes to that of a storm-tossed sky. Marcy had cut deep scars into his soul, and he'd sworn he'd never let it happen again. But now, Jessie was a big believer in love.

Even though Kurt was across the room, his gaze locked on her. The look he gave her sizzled with expectation. And she suddenly couldn't wait for the honeymoon.

The band struck up another song and Nick kept hold of her.

"Sorry to cut in," Kurt said seconds later, his tone containing no contrition.

Nick grinned at Kurt, then at her. "No problem. I was just going to ask someone else to dance."

"You do that," Kurt said.

"Kurt!" Jessie protested in shock. Another new side to the man she loved. She wondered how much more discovery was ahead. And she looked forward to every moment of it.

"Lillian's a great dancer," Kurt said.

"Lillian Baldwin?" Nick echoed, his gaze searching her out.

"And she did a great job on the flowers," Jessie added.

With a warning not to do anything on their honeymoon that he wouldn't do, Nick headed to the punch bowl, where, Jessie noticed, Lillian stood, sipping from a glass and looking at the bouquet she'd somehow caught.

"Think it's time we left," Kurt said.

"But we just got here."

"And your point is?"

She traced a finger across his lips, not caring that half the people in the reception hall were staring at them. Dressed in a black tux, tie and cummerbund, polished boots and a new Stetson, Kurt stole her breath.

She'd never seen him in a jacket before and marveled at the way his shoulders stretched the material wide. He was every inch an attractive male, every inch her husband. She was so happy, she was tempted to pinch herself. How was it possible for any woman to be so happy?

"How 'bout it, Jess, want to run away from your party?"

"Thought I'd get one last dance from you before we left."

He shook his head. "I'll dance with you all night, but not here. When we're alone—when I can hold you the way I want to without fear of giving Mrs. Johnson a heart attack."

"Oh." He caught her finger in his mouth. When he suckled, her knees sank forward. "Let's, er, yes, we should..."

"Good. I was hoping I wouldn't have to toss you over my shoulder." His voice was husky and edgy, saying he'd run out of patience. "All this lace and froufrou would make it impossible to see."

She pretended indignation. "I love this dress."

"I love what's underneath it. Come on, Jess, take pity on your groom." He caught her free hand and stroked his thumb across the golden band that he'd slipped on her finger just an hour ago, joining them together for a lifetime.

"Let's go," she said.

He grinned and his dark green eyes lightened like rain on a blade of grass.

Kurt's attempt to sneak them out failed.

As they headed for the door, murmurs ran through the crowd. Mary, along with Kurt's parents, hurried over. Mary took Jessie's hands and welcomed her to the family.

For a moment, Jessie couldn't speak. She had a family, a real family, a place to spend the holidays, a place that warmed and welcomed. *She had a family.* And she marveled at the wonder of it all.

Less than five seconds later, she was enfolded in a hug, support and caring surrounding her. She hadn't counted on this part of her dreams coming true. She'd wanted a family like Kurt's and now they'd embraced her as one of their own.

Tears blurred her vision again, for the dozenth time that day.

Kurt promised that they would visit after their honeymoon and proprietorially placed his fingertips in the small of her back.

"You'd better go, young lady," Ray Majors urged while draping an arm around his wife's shoulders, "while my son is still being polite."

In Ray and Alice, Jessie caught a glimpse of her future, imagining herself and Kurt at their son's or daughter's wedding.

The kind of love she and Kurt shared was made of the same stuff as his parents', and that meant it was a forever love.

Outside, she laughed at the sight of Kurt's pickup truck, tin cans hanging from the bumper, Just Married stenciled in several different places and a lasso hanging from the rearview mirror. "I guess this means someone thinks I roped the roping champion."

"Nah." He tipped back his hat to look at her. "Means I finally roped the biggest prize of all."

Then, taking off his hat and using it to shield them from view, if not from catcalls and cheers, he kissed her.

As guests rained birdseed on them, Kurt lifted Jessie and slid her on to the pickup's seat, stealing a peek at her ankle and calf in payment.

She wondered if her red face clashed with her white lace hat.

Going around to the other side, he climbed in, gave her a promising look, turned the ignition, then headed out of town.

When they'd left the outskirts of Columbine Crossing in a cloud of dust, he pulled over to the side of the road. "Alone, finally."

She didn't protest when he pulled her against him, knocking off his hat.

The kiss he claimed left her dizzy with anticipation. It was a heady mixture of possessiveness and promise. She felt cherished.

Reality certainly surpassed her imagination.

He deepened the kiss and she slid her hands around him, feeling his strength and inhaling his heat.

When he finally released her, her shoulders drooped forward. She would never get enough of him.

"I...I need to tell you something," she said. Now that confession time was here, her mouth had dried.

"Go on."

"About our honeymoon..."

"Yes?" He stroked his knuckles down the side of her face, reaching to pull the pins from her hair. "I've wanted to do this all day."

"I've wanted it, too."

Feathering his fingers into her loosened hair, he asked, "What's your deep, dark secret?"

His other hand had started down her throat, dipping into the cleavage of her gown...

"Hmm?"

"I'm...I can't think."

"Sorry." He didn't stop.

"I need to tell you that I've canceled our airline reservations."

That cinched his interest.

"I'm...kidnapping you."

His brow raised and his hands finally stilled.

"I rented us a cabin."

"So there're no other people around?"

"Right."

"I like it already." Leaning toward her, he moistened her earlobe with his tongue.

This close, surely he heard and saw the pounding of her pulse in her throat. And she knew he had to be aware that she'd become supple in his arms as resistance fled and want rushed in.

"Is there more?" he asked against her ear.

Thought all but vanished.

"Hmm, Jess?"

He made her weak. "I left our clothes behind."

He stared at her, his look of hunger turning ravenous.

He *was* ravenous.

He wanted her, with a need that increased every day.

She'd come into her own, he realized. And he liked it.

A month ago, she hadn't known she possessed this kind of feminine power. But now she did, and she had it in championship quantities. It had been there all along, but she'd finally found the courage to explore it. Ugly duckling? No way. His Jessie dazzled even the most beautiful of swans. Lucky for him. She was a marvel.

She was his.

Life, he decided, didn't get any better than this.

"As for the kidnapping..." he started to say.

She swallowed, her columbine blue eyes blossoming.

"The sooner you kidnap me, the better."

He obviously had a few more things to learn about her. A lifetime wouldn't be enough, he knew, but it was a start.

"Kurt..."

He placed a kiss on her temple, then moved down, kissing the area right above the neckline of her dress.

"I'm kidnapping *you*."

"So you are."

Turning tables, she leaned into him, pushing against his chest, moving him away and gently shoving him backward until he rested against the door.

This was a new Jessie.

Definitely a new Jessie. Suddenly it felt a whole lot hotter than the weatherman promised for Kurt's wedding day.

Gown and all, she shimmied onto his lap, tangled her fingers in his hair and kissed him so deeply his head spun.

Then, against his mouth, she whispered a wicked suggestion.

"You want me to what?" he demanded, then grinned, only too happy to oblige her.

No, a lifetime of loving her wouldn't be enough, not nearly enough.

* * * * *

If you enjoyed what you just read,
then we've got an offer you can't resist!

Take 2 bestselling love stories FREE!

Plus get a FREE surprise gift!

Clip this page and mail it to Silhouette Reader Service™

IN U.S.A.	IN CANADA
3010 Walden Ave.	P.O. Box 609
P.O. Box 1867	Fort Erie, Ontario
Buffalo, N.Y. 14240-1867	L2A 5X3

YES! Please send me 2 free Silhouette Desire® novels and my free surprise gift. Then send me 6 brand-new novels every month, which I will receive months before they're available in stores. In the U.S.A., bill me at the bargain price of $3.12 plus 25¢ delivery per book and applicable sales tax, if any*. In Canada, bill me at the bargain price of $3.49 plus 25¢ delivery per book and applicable taxes**. That's the complete price and a savings of over 10% off the cover prices—what a great deal! I understand that accepting the 2 free books and gift places me under no obligation ever to buy any books. I can always return a shipment and cancel at any time. Even if I never buy another book from Silhouette, the 2 free books and gift are mine to keep forever. So why not take us up on our invitation. You'll be glad you did!

225 SEN CNFA
326 SEN CNFC

Name	(PLEASE PRINT)	
Address	Apt.#	
City	State/Prov.	Zip/Postal Code

* Terms and prices subject to change without notice. Sales tax applicable in N.Y.
** Canadian residents will be charged applicable provincial taxes and GST.
  All orders subject to approval. Offer limited to one per household.
  ® are registered trademarks of Harlequin Enterprises Limited.

DES99   ©1998 Harlequin Enterprises Limited

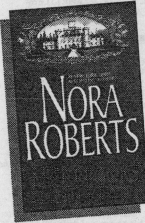
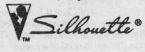

COMING NEXT MONTH